# SAVED BY THE BIG BAD WOLF

A Darkhills Romance

Elizabeth Greene

*Happy Reading
Elizabeth Greene
x*

Copyright © 2020 Elizabeth Greene

All rights reserved

The characters and events portrayed in this book are fictitious. Any similarity to real persons, living or dead, is coincidental and not intended by the author.

No part of this book may be reproduced, or stored in a retrieval system, or transmitted in any form or by any means, electronic, mechanical, photocopying, recording, or otherwise, without express written permission of the publisher.

ISBN-13: 9798566445359

Cover design by: Elizabeth Greene

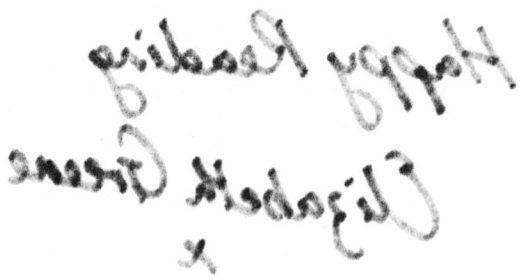

*For my beloved sister*
x

# CONTENTS

Title Page
Copyright
Dedication

| | |
|---|---:|
| CHAPTER ONE | 1 |
| CHAPTER TWO | 9 |
| CHAPTER THREE | 28 |
| CHAPTER FOUR | 40 |
| CHAPTER FIVE | 51 |
| CHAPTER SIX | 57 |
| CHAPTER SEVEN | 69 |
| CHAPTER EIGHT | 81 |
| CHAPTER NINE | 100 |
| CHAPTER TEN | 106 |
| CHAPTER ELEVEN | 114 |
| CHAPTER TWELVE | 129 |
| CHAPTER THIRTEEN | 146 |
| CHAPTER FOURTEEN | 158 |
| CHAPTER FIFTEEN | 163 |
| CHAPTER SIXTEEN | 168 |
| CHAPTER SEVENTEEN | 180 |

| | |
|---|---|
| CHAPTER EIGHTEEN | 193 |
| CHAPTER NINETEEN | 206 |
| CHAPTER TWENTY | 218 |
| CHAPTER TWENTY-ONE | 231 |
| CHAPTER TWENTY-TWO | 249 |
| EPILOGUE | 263 |
| Thank you | 271 |
| Books In This Series | 273 |
| Sneak Preview: | 287 |

# CHAPTER ONE

*Cayden*

Damn, it's been a hot one today.

Cayden Greystone cursed as he loaded up the back of his truck at the end of his shift. He swiped the sweat from his brow and not for the first time this summer, considered whether he should shave his beard already. The sun had already begun its descent in the sky, yet it was still as hot as Satan's stove. The mosquitoes were starting to get too familiar and all Cayden wanted was a cold shower and an even colder beer.

The rest of the crew had long clocked off for the day, leaving him to bring down the last tree on the day's quota on his own. He'd brought it down easy enough, now all that remained was to heft the felled pine onto the stack ready for removal tomorrow. He had long gotten used to this routine. It was the same wherever he sought work, he was the outsider so didn't get the privileges that members of the pack received. If he wanted to earn his money, he needed to put in the hours.

This past week he didn't even blame the other wolves for their eagerness to get the hell out of the stifling mugginess of the forest. He might be the type that kept his thoughts to himself, but that didn't mean he didn't hear the murmurs of discontent. They were tired, unmotivated and struggling to earn the wages they needed to improve their quality of living for their mates and families. He'd heard the same last summer and it appeared that nothing had changed, if anything the situation had gotten worse. It was something that seemed out of kilter with the flashy trucks that the Alpha and Beta drove around the territory.

Cayden suspected that something was amiss and if it were his pack, he wouldn't be happy seeing his people at a disadvantage while *he* had access to luxury. But not all packs believed in sharing resources fairly and it wasn't his place to investigate or ask questions, despite the niggling feeling in his gut that told him to make it right.

It was the Alpha in him. The instinct to protect and support the other wolves around him was ingrained. He wasn't an Alpha though; he didn't have a pack. Not anymore. So, he told himself it was none of his business and kept his keen nose out.

While he wouldn't do anything about the

situation, he could empathize. He couldn't hold it against the other wolves on the crew for feeling discontented and unmotivated. They seemed like a good-hearted, honest crew and if he were a pack member, he would've joined them for a trip into the town for a quiet beer in the local bar to dull the feeling of hopelessness.

Especially if *she* was working that evening. The beautiful she-wolf with the dark reddish-brown hair and eyes that felt like his very soul was held in her grasp.

Cayden shook his head and reminded himself not to get any ideas. He was a lone wolf and as such, was not allowed to mix with the females of the pack; especially the unmated ones. He was entitled to buy whatever he needed from the town but fraternizing with the townsfolk, especially the females, was off-limits.

He got it: females were coveted. Packs would allow matings with other packs if they were on friendly terms, but lone wolves were considered an unpredictable threat. However, he was strong and hardworking, and so they didn't mind employing him for the odd contract here or there, just so long as he kept it in his pants.

Usually, that wasn't a problem, there had always been enough human women who had willingly taken him to their beds when he needed to scratch that particular itch, but *this* female was something else. There was a reason other than the seasonal paycheck that ensured he returned to this town each summer. The female was too intriguing to shake from his mind. Despite knowing he would never be worthy of any female, never be able to offer her the support and stability that she would need, he kept coming back.

The first summer he had met her, he had been running wild through the forest, his wolf enjoying the lush surroundings and tough terrain. He'd stopped at a stream to drink and there she'd been, watching him with those crisp green eyes that had haunted his dreams ever since. Fast forward to last summer and they had spent almost every night in their wolf forms, never shifting to see their human form. They didn't need to, the companionship they had shared as they'd exhausted themselves on their daily sprints had forged a strong connection.

This year, he had returned, desperate for another stolen moment with the female that he could never have, fearful that he would find her finally mated. To his disappointment, Cayden had not seen her in the forest yet, but her scent lingered faintly at a large cabin in the woods where an elder female wolf lived. His wolf ran past it every evening in the hope of catching her there: searching for the prize that was not to be his. Clearly, he was a glutton for punishment. All he ever found was the elderly lady, sitting on the porch, watching him with barely concealed amusement.

Cayden had finally seen his mystery she-wolf in town the night before. He had driven in to pick up groceries and had followed his nose against his better judgment. He knew he shouldn't be following the scent of any female, but he had scented her the moment he had gotten out of his truck and his instincts had overridden his sensibility. She had been busy emptying trash into the dumpster out the back of the local bar, her back to him. Then, as though she had sensed him too, she'd turned, and their eyes had locked with an intensity that had caused every muscle in his body to throb with need.

He had stood rooted to the spot, mentally fighting against his wolf as it scratched and clawed at him to move towards the female. She was the most beautiful creature he had ever seen. Petite yet curvy, with lush red lips, glossy mahogany hair that fell about her shoulders in wild, thick curls, and her eyes were the same mesmerizing green as her animal. He could scent her wolf within. Could practically hear her whining to him. She was still unmated. He couldn't fathom why such a strong she-wolf hadn't been claimed. Her pheromones were off the scale and if he didn't know any better, he would've thought her an Alpha female.

Cayden had been relieved when she had slowly backed away into the bar once more, never taking her eyes from his. If she had turned her back on him, he wasn't sure if he could've contained his wolf. The instinct to hunt its prey would've been too great. He had no right to even scent her, let alone act upon his animal instincts towards the female. He was a lone wolf: she was off limits.

Cayden shook himself from the memory again, his wolf pacing deep inside. He should know better than to revisit that moment. He should know better than to keep running in the forest in the hope of finding her, so they could run free again. Yet he couldn't stop himself from wanting another moment with the only other wolf that he had felt a connection to ever since leaving his pack.

And that was where his musings needed to end.

He slammed the back of his truck shut and marched around to the cab, climbing in. He didn't have connections. He didn't have a pack. He never would. It was better that way.

Resigning himself to another solitary night, Cayden turned the ignition and drove along the winding forest track in the direction of his trailer. He didn't mind being so far from the town, he honestly preferred living among nature. It gave his wolf easy access to roam and in a world where shifters and paranormal creatures were still considered legends from fairy tales, it was for the best that his wolf could run free without the risk of being discovered.

The night-time bugs and critters were busy making a racket by the time he climbed out of his truck and unlocked the door to his trailer. It wasn't huge. Hell, it wasn't even big, he had to keep his six-foot-five frame hunched over whenever he was inside, but it had all a bachelor like him needed. A bed-come-couch, a small shower room, a kitchenette and a TV.

He ducked his head as he stepped inside. The confined space drew a sigh from him. He'd make up one of the instant ramen dinners he'd picked up from town the night before, grab a quick shower and crack open a beer before turning in for the night. His gaze flicked to the compact bed that was a mess of rumpled sheets. It was hardly inviting. Then again, he knew his dreams would be filled with images of the she-wolf. Cayden smiled at the prospect. Although it would be bittersweet, it would be the highlight of his night. But before he gave in to any of that, it was time for a run.

He shucked out of his boots and dusty work clothes and shifted as he stepped down from the trailer, back outside into the warm evening. Smooth, tanned skin transformed into thick, dark fur, his face lengthened, and his teeth sharpened as lean muscles contracted and morphed Cayden's body from human into animal. His paws landed with soft thuds on the hard forest floor. He shook out his aching limbs, stretching and rolling in the cool, dry dirt. It felt good to be back on four legs. The woody scent of pine and damp moss assaulted his nose and the sounds of the nocturnal animals waking and moving around the dusky forest intensified in his ears. Cayden's wolf smiled, teeth gleaming and tongue tasting the air. This was what he needed. This was where he belonged. Just him, his wolf and the forest.

In a flash of ebony fur and amber eyes, he disappeared into the trees.

# CHAPTER TWO

## *Rose*

"Yeesh, it's slow in here tonight." Rose's friend and fellow bartender complained as she wiped down the bar top for the umpteenth time. "I'll do another tour of the place to collect empties then I might take another break to call Clint. Nothing much else to do."

Rose smiled at her friend's comments, she was right. Tonight *had* been dead. Only a few of the regulars were still hanging about the place, nursing a bottle of beer or a bowl of nuts. No one could afford a big night out, so nights like this had become the norm.

"Don't sweat it, take your break. I'll sweep the tables and see if anyone needs anything else. It'd be good if we could close up early." Rose offered.

"Thanks, hon, an early finish would be great. Clint's been so tired lately, by the time I get home he's always snoring his head off. I keep trying to tell him that we ain't gonna make any cubs just by holding hands." Carly wagged her eyebrows and smiled mischievously as she grabbed her phone and headed out back, her long blonde hair swishing behind her.

Rose chuckled at her friend. On the one hand, she thought it was the cutest thing that Carly was so desperate to start a family, but on the other hand, she worried that she was putting a strain on her husband.

They weren't long mated and usually, a male wolf couldn't wait to knock up his female. But Clint was making excuses. She knew he couldn't be that tired. A male wolf was *never* too tired to satisfy his mate. She had been in the same class in school as Clint and knew him to be one of the most conscientious and sensible wolves in the pack. She suspected that the real reason was that Clint was worried about being able to afford to have cubs.

Everyone in town was feeling the pinch. Wages had been declining in the past few years, but things still cost the same. At first, it hadn't been too noticeable; people tightened their belts and made do. But recently it had been taking its toll. Rose wondered if the Alpha and Beta knew how bad things had gotten. Then again, she had noticed a few anomalies in the accounts for the bar, rent to the Alpha had been higher than usual, increasing almost every month. Perhaps even he was feeling the pinch, although you wouldn't have thought it by the lavishness of his home in town or the shine on his new truck.

Something was going on, but Rose couldn't prove much, nor was she in a position to raise her concerns with the Alpha or Beta. She was an oddity in the pack. Not really a full member but one of them, nonetheless.

Rose had belonged to another pack; she was the first-born female of the Alpha couple. When an aggressive leadership challenge had been made, she was sent to her mother's parents for safe keeping. Her parents had been confident that the challenge would be dealt with quickly and everything would return to normal. However, things didn't work out that way and by age three, Rose had found herself orphaned, unable to return to her pack and adopted by her grandparents.

The Alpha at the time had welcomed her into the pack, there was a blood bond through her maternal line after all, but it was under the proviso that when she was of age, she would need to consummate her membership to the pack through mating with one of the pack's males. With no other options, her grandparents had agreed to the terms. Mating with a male from your pack was deemed normal and they supposed she would fall for someone as she grew into womanhood.

However, her coming of age had long since passed and Rose hadn't felt the mating urge with any of the males in the pack. She liked plenty of them. Had even shared naive fledgling kisses with some of them during high school but none had called to her wolf. Clearly, none of them had been interested in *her* either as she had watched the males pair off with other females and start growing their own families.

Time had ticked on; the old Alpha had passed, and his only son had stepped into the role while Rose had been a young teenager. She had grown to be such a part of the pack, a beloved friend to all, that nobody had mentioned the caveat of her needing to mate in order to stay. Either that or they were all too respectful, or terrified, of her battle axe of a grandmother to say anything.

That was until a year ago.

Since her grandfather passed away, her bond to the pack had become even more tenuous. Her grandfather had been a deeply respected member of the pack, a good friend to the former Alpha, and her grandmother still held a position of respectable status. However, Judy Woods was getting older and frailer. Rose didn't know how much longer she would be around before she joined her mate in the afterlife. Without her grandmother, she would have no living blood bond to the pack. She'd have friends and those who loved her like family, but blood was blood. And in wolf society, blood and mating were everything.

Rose hadn't been the only one to realise her position within the pack was under threat. The Alpha, Samuel Wyatt McClaw, had noticed too. For the past year, he had been subtly raising the subject with her. At first, it had been friendly enquiries as to whether he would need to officiate any mating ceremonies in the near future, but more recently it had turned into directly asking her on dates or fabricating reasons for the two of them to be alone together.

The Alpha's previous mate had left him, and they had never been successful in producing cubs. It was also unspoken knowledge among the pack that his mate had found another male a few states over.

Rose understood his desire to secure his leadership by mating and producing an heir. He was getting older, so she supposed he felt that time was running out for him and perhaps he was lonely. However, he was technically old enough to be her father and not only did he make her skin crawl, but her wolf outright growled at the thought of being mated to him.

Any suspicions she had that he was messing with the bar's finances and taking profits that weren't rightfully his, had to be kept to herself. If she wanted any chance of staying in the town she loved, she couldn't challenge the Alpha.

Rose had thought of speaking to the Beta about her concerns, Russell had always been sweet and friendly towards her. Everyone liked Russell and he was often the good cop to the Alpha's bad cop routine. But considering he was also driving around in a brand-new truck and wore the *only* designer clothes ever spotted in the town, she couldn't help but wonder if he too had been benefiting from the Alpha's skimming off the books.

As Rose collected the few remaining empty bottles from the deserted tables she sighed heavily. She loved the people in this town, those who weren't shifters were aware and respectful of the pack. Families were close and everyone looked out for each other. As the last remaining customers rose from their seats and shuffled towards the exit, she received warm bear hugs from each of them and waved them off with a genuine smile. She sure would miss this town if she were forced to leave.

Just as she was about to lock the door and set about cleaning down, the door swung open and a pale-faced, haggard-looking man burst into the bar, his tan-coloured trench coat hung unevenly off one shoulder. Rose plastered on a pleasant smile, even though the last thing she wanted was to have to stay open and chew the fat with a stranger.

Especially one that made her inner wolf crack open a watchful eye. However, he smelt entirely human so didn't pose much of a threat to her.

"We were just closing for the night; can I help you with anything before we do?" She asked.

"I need a whiskey and directions." The man sat himself down on one of the bar stools and slid a few dollars across the bar towards her.

The money was barely enough for a drink of soda but considering everyone was broke these days, she decided to be kind and serve the man his drink. The sweat and anxiety pouring off him gave the impression that he *really* needed it.

She poured him a measure of the cheapest house whiskey and punched the sale into the register, depositing the few dollars.

"You ain't from around here, where are you heading?" She asked over her shoulder.

The man downed his whiskey at an alarming speed and dropped the glass back on the counter with a thud.

"Tumbricane Manor. You heard of it? Half these roads ain't even marked in this godforsaken Hicksville. I gotta be there tonight."

The man shoved his glass forward and nodded at the bottle behind Rose, she put down the glass she had been wiping and folded her arms. She wasn't about to give him another handout, she'd been generous enough to give him his first drink for half price. That, combined with his insulting attitude to her beloved town, hadn't exactly made her warm to him.

"I know of Tumbricane, can't say I've ever been there but I roughly know where it is."

The guy was from out of town and human therefore, most likely had no idea of the paranormal world that existed alongside his own. She wasn't about to tell him she knew it from her runs in the forest but not by the roads on the map. So, she would have to give him rough directions.

"Well, you got a map or something? I ain't got all night Missy."

Rose's wolf stood up at that, extending her claws as she stretched. The guy was an offensive asshole and she wanted him out of her bar. Rose grabbed the out-of-date map that sat propped up behind the cash register and flicked to the right page.

"Here. If you follow this road out of town and take the left turning here," She pointed to the map so that the man could see, "Then keep heading towards the mountains you should find it. No-one else lives up that way so the most well-taken track will likely take you to Tumbricane."

"Is that it? Is that the best you can do?" The guy snarled at her, sweat showing on his brow, his eyes bloodshot.

*Sheesh, he's in bad shape.*

Rose could scent his panic heavily. Whatever business he had at Tumbricane with its mysterious owner, she did not want to know. Her wolf's hackles were up, and she wanted the guy gone.

"Like I said," Rose took the map back from his grasp. "I've never visited. I only know of it. Those are your directions: take 'em or leave 'em."

"I'm gonna be taking that map."

"No, you will not. Now I'm afraid I'm going to have to ask you to leave, we're closed now," Rose said firmly.

"Now listen here you little bitch—"

The man didn't get a chance to utter another word. Samuel McClaw had entered the bar and had grabbed the man by the scruff of his collar, lifting him off his bar stool. He wasn't the biggest wolf in the pack, despite being the Alpha, but he was strong and enjoyed any opportunity to demonstrate the fact.

"The only little bitch around here is you. Now apologize to the lady and get out of my town." The Alpha growled out.

"Fuck, I ain't got time for this shit." The pale, sweaty man said, more frustrated than scared. "I'm sorry. Now can you let go of me so I can get the hell out of here?"

Sam glared at the man but released him after another moment of attempting to intimidate him. Rose inwardly cursed as the man scurried out of the bar, his long trench coat flapping behind him. She had the situation under control, she was a strong female, capable of landing that guy on his ass before he even had a chance to notice, but instead, she had been 'rescued' by the Alpha.

After watching the man leave, Sam turned back to face Rose with a look of manly pride on his face. His shoulders were pulled back to puff out his chest. Making the buttons on his flannel shirt strain. He wasn't a completely unattractive male, but his arrogance and bullying nature soured any charm Rose might have found in his appearance.

"It's a good thing I decided to swing by," He said.

"Yeah thanks, Sam. He wouldn't have been around for much longer anyway, but I'm glad he's gone," Rose replied, trying her best to seem grateful to her Alpha.

"You see, this is exactly what I wanted to talk to you about." His brow furrowed under his baseball cap, his gray eyes darkening as he prepared to launch into what she knew was coming: the attempt to persuade her that she needed a man. And that man; should be him.

"You really should consider my offer, Rosie."

She hated him calling her that. She was Rose. *Not* Rosie. Sam deciding on a pet name for her didn't make them closer in any way shape or form.

"It's obvious that you are vulnerable without having a male in your life to protect you. There is no-one better than the Alpha to do that for you, and I think I proved my point just now." He stood with his legs apart and hands on his hips as if to make it clear that he wasn't taking no for an answer. Too bad he would have to.

"Sam, it really is very considerate of you to want to make sure I'm taken care of. You've known me since I was a kid and it's nice to know that you're looking out for me," Rose always tried to remind him of their age difference in the hope that it would put him off, she liked to think that it had helped keep him at bay so far. "But I'm doing okay. Me and Gran look out for each other and I've got good friends in this town."

"And what happens when you go home to your

apartment at night Rosie? Who's taken care of you then?" Sam pressed.

The implication of her needing him to take care of her in more ways than one made her skin crawl. She chose to act dumb and ignore it.

"I have great neighbours and—"

"Sooner or later you are gonna find yourself all alone, and without any blood tie to this pack, I'm going to have no choice but to force you to leave. I don't want that for you, Rosie, I'm offering you the chance to lead this pack with me. Move out of that tiny apartment that you're renting and settle yourself in my home. You'd want for nothing and I'd make sure that your grandmother saw out the rest of her days in the best old folks' home in town."

Rose was furious. He'd never been so blunt before and the way he had moved forward to lean across the bar at her made her inner wolf start to bristle. She opened her mouth to refuse him but was cut off by his rough fingers pressed against her lips. It took every ounce of self-control not to bite the presumptuous Alpha.

"Think about it darlin'. Your grandma probably ain't long for this world, which means you are running out of time. The hospitality of this pack ain't going to last after she's gone. Do you really want your grandmother's last thoughts to be filled with worrying about you? Hell, I'm surprised she ain't dropped dead from worrying over you already."

At that, a growl slipped past Rose's lips. If he weren't the Alpha, she'd already be at his throat.

"Or do you want that sweet, kind lady, who took you in and raised you when no-one else would, to go to meet her mate knowing you were safe and taken care of by the finest male in town?"

Finest male in town, her ass.

"My grandmother loves me." Rose bit out. "She would want me to make my mating choice with my own free will. She would want me to answer the mating call of the wolf who was fated for me, just as she did and just as my mother did."

"And look how well that turned out for your mother." Sam drawled sadistically.

Rose gasped. She had never seen this vicious and manipulative side of the Alpha before. She'd heard he was mean when he wanted to be, but he'd never shown it to a female as far as she knew. Then again, his mate had left him, it wouldn't have been without reason.

"Hey Sam, whatcha doing here? Its good to see you." Carly chose that moment to come bounding in from where she'd been on the phone to her mate out back.

The Alpha's frame relaxed instantly, and an easy smile spread over his rough, stubbled face.

"Oh, hey there Carly girl, how are you and Clint getting along?"

"We're doing real good, we're fixing up our little home, hoping to welcome some little paws someday." She beamed back at him.

"Well now, that sounds like you two have your hands full. Tell you what, why don't you and Clint take it easy on Saturday night and join Rosie and me for some good, old-fashioned steak and beers?"

Rose cursed the manipulative bastard. Carly's face lit up at the prospect of a night out, mixing with the Alpha no less. How could she deny her friends a chance to potentially climb the ranks of the pack? The increased social standing might result in better wages for Clint, and then getting pregnant might be back on the cards for the couple.

"Oh wow, Sam, that sounds great."

"Good, good. My treat you understand." He waggled a good-natured finger at the buoyant woman, his laughing gray eyes lit with victory. "Rosie here has told me all about how hard you two have been working on the house and Clint's efforts at the timber yard haven't gone unnoticed."

"Well, thank you, Sam. Thank you very much, I can't wait to go home and tell Clint."

"Perfect, Rose and I will meet you at Ray's Steakhouse at eight on Saturday. I'll see you then."

Sam made a show of taking off his baseball cap and bowed towards Rose in what she guessed he must've intended as a gentlemanly gesture. All it did was showcase his increasing bald spot; yet another reminder that he was old enough to be her father.

"I'll pick you up from your place, Rosie. I sure can't wait to see you all dolled up."

Rose had no answer for that. So, she grit her teeth behind a closed-lipped smile and nodded before turning her back to wipe down the tables. She heard him leave to a jubilant farewell from Carly. As soon as his truck roared to life and the sound of crunching tyres indicated he'd gone, Rose went to the door and locked it.

"Can you believe that?" Carly said.

"Nope."

"Me and Clint are double dating with the Alpha! When were you gonna tell me you'd finally decided to give him a shot?" Her friend teased.

"I haven't. He just arranged that whole thing

without even asking me." Rose stated angrily.

"You serious? Why would he do that?"

"Because he knew I wouldn't agree to it without putting me on the spot like that."

"Like what?" Carly asked, confused.

"By making it impossible for me to say no. There's no way I'd ruin the chance for you and Clint to have a night out and rub shoulders with the Alpha. This could be a big deal for you two."

"Hey now, Rose, if you don't wanna go, then we won't go. Me and Clint get by just fine. A night out eating steak and drinking beer would be swell and all but not if it means putting you in an awkward situation." Carly took hold of Rose's hands and squeezed them tight.

Rose loved her friends. She wanted what was best for them. Maybe one date with Sam wouldn't be so bad. Maybe then he'd see that she wasn't a good mate for him, that they had nothing in common and he'd finally leave her alone. In the meantime, she'd speak with her grandma tomorrow. She had tried not to concern her with the issues she was having with the Alpha, but it was time she sought out her sage advice.

"No, no. It won't be awkward. It'll be fine. I think Sam is just trying to convince himself that we'd be good together. It isn't going to happen, but a night of dinner and drinks with you and Clint won't do any harm. Let's do it."

"You sure?" Carly asked.

Rose could tell she was holding her excitement in as best she could, but the corners of her friend's mouth were twitching upwards.

"Yes, let's do it. Besides, it's free right?"

"Oh, hell yes!" Carly grinned and hugged Rose tight, making her smile indulgently.

Meanwhile, her wolf paced uneasily, snorting her disapproval. Her animal didn't want to be anywhere near the Alpha. She knew who she wanted to be near and whimpered with longing. But Rose knew it couldn't happen.

Lone wolves were notoriously bad news. She didn't necessarily believe that to be true, but the fact remained that he was off limits or she might as well leave her grandmother and the town she loved behind, right then and there. Her time with the alluring lone wolf was best left in the past, with memories of last summer's exhilarating night-time runs, and delicious dreams of how he had looked at her with so much dangerous promise the night before. She'd never felt anything so powerful before in her life. Her body shivered just thinking about him and her inner wolf sighed dramatically as she rolled onto her back with a wicked twinkle in her eye.

*Such a hussy*, Rose thought, smiling to herself.

She finished shutting down the bar for the night and waved goodbye to Carly as she climbed into her beloved old jeep. It had been her grandfather's and although it had seen better days, it was still going strong. She looked at the time on the dashboard. It was too late to visit her grandmother now; she'd be in bed already. Most likely having fallen asleep reading one of her romance novels. Rose chuckled to herself at the thought. The tough, no-nonsense woman would never admit to enjoying the books, but Rose had found more than a couple of them lying around the house whenever she had visited.

Despite what the old battle axe would have you believe, Rose knew her grandmother had a soft heart, *lived* for happily ever after and was a firm believer in true love conquering all. Maybe she'd pick up a new book from the local goodwill store tomorrow morning before she headed over to see her. Rose would just slip it under the TV Guide and let the old romantic find it in her own time.

With a lumbering chug of the engine, Rose headed towards her apartment. She would try to put thoughts of the propositioning Alpha out of her mind until she visited with her grandmother tomorrow. Tonight, she would get some rest and maybe indulge in a little dreaming of a certain forbidden wolf with piercing amber eyes.

# CHAPTER THREE

## *Cayden*

Cayden felt the sweat trickle down the side of his face as he lifted one end of the giant pine they had just taken down. This one was so big it took three of them to lift and load it onto the nearby logging truck. It would've been easier if they had been a crew of four, but the Beta of the pack hadn't arrived for his shift yet. From the grumblings of the other wolves, it was apparent that this was a regular occurrence. It was also unusual that he never saw any bear shifters brought in as extra labour. They'd make light work of the huge pines. Then again bears were known to be none too fond of wolves, and they were expensive to hire.

It didn't bother Cayden too much. The extra strain on his muscles was a welcome distraction from thoughts of the she-wolf. She'd haunted his dreams again last night and while he had enjoyed them at the time, it had left him feeling needy and unfulfilled when he'd woken with the dawn. The obsession was becoming all-consuming, if it continued to escalate, he'd have to quit his contract early and get the hell out of there.

The other scenario saw him seeking her out, rules be damned. She didn't need that kind of trouble and nor did he. So, Cayden focused on the heavy pull on his arms and back and grunted with the effort it took to heft the felled giant up and onto the truck bed.

Task completed, the three men, stomped over to where their pick-ups were parked. They'd earned a five-minute break.

"Fuck, today's feeling long already," one of the wolves said with a huff.

He was a lean and muscular man with rich brown hair who was always chatting. Cayden liked the guy's sense of humour and found he enjoyed listening to his commentaries on their daily slog.

"I don't mind it," said the other male, he was a bigger, broader wolf with light sandy hair and quiet, easy-going nature. "Means I don't have to fake feeling tired tonight."

That piqued Cayden's curiosity. The wolf was newly mated and should be right in the midst of his honeymoon period; he should be *arriving* at work exhausted instead of going home that way.

"You still keeping up that old charade?" The first wolf asked, "I don't know how you do it, if I had a mate like Carly—"

A low warning growl emitted from the other wolf.

"You keep your ideas about my mate to yourself or I'll ensure you regret it, Nate."

"Easy, Clint, easy." The first wolf held up his hands in a surrendering gesture. "I said, 'like Carly' not actually Carly."

Clint's growl grew louder, his muscles tensing underneath his loose vest. Cayden cursed inwardly. He'd have to do some peacekeeping if the male wouldn't shut up about the other's mate. Wolves were extremely protective of their mates and wouldn't stand for others openly admiring them.

"I'd stop saying the female's name for a start, Nate, or you're going to get your ass kicked," Cayden said, stepping up beside Clint, and handing him a bottle of water, hoping to cool his temper.

"Ah shit, I'm sorry. I didn't mean anything by it. All I mean is, it must be killing you, going home each night and lying to her. How can you do it?" Nate visibly slumped his posture in submission to Clint.

It was funny, Cayden would've assumed by their contrasting personalities that the hierarchy between them would've been the other way around. Seeing the gesture, Clint relaxed and opened the bottle of water, chugging half the contents down. Cayden grabbed another bottle and lightly tossed it to Nate. Crisis averted. Although something was clearly not right there.

"Of course it's killing me. Hell, I've spent my whole damn life thinking about building a home with my mate, raising a family, living the good life." Clint finished his water and tossed the empty bottle into the back of his pick-up. "But how can I do that when we're barely making enough money to keep the roof over our heads. I can't raise a family knowing they'll be hungry, and every day will be a struggle. I can't do that to Carly."

He bowed his head and took off his baseball cap to run his hand through his sweat-dampened hair.

Cayden's gut twisted. He had no idea that the situation was so bad within the pack. He earned enough from his various contracts to keep himself comfortable, but then he supposed he had no dependents, no family and he lived in a tiny trailer which he owned outright. His wolf stirred inside him, rising to its feet. Cayden felt uncomfortable and the need to offer support thronged deeply through his veins. He shook his head and clapped a hand on Clint's shoulder.

"I'm sorry man," he murmured.

"Ain't you going out with the Alpha this week though? Couldn't you ask him for a pay rise?" Nate pitched in.

"Don't remind me," Clint replied, fidgeting with his cap. "Carly's so excited; thinks this means our problems are solved. Honestly, I wish we didn't have to sit through an evening with him while he creeps on Rose, and I ain't so sure I'd like to earn my money the way the Alpha does business."

Cayden removed his hand and stepped back casually. This definitely was not his place. Hearing the Alpha wasn't acting in an honourable way put his wolf's hackles all the way up and he needed to remind himself that this wasn't his pack, and therefore was not his problem.

"Yeah, I see your point. I don't like the way he is with her. I've known her since kindergarten, she's a good female."

"Yeah, she is. So why don't you ask her out instead?" Clint perked up at the possibility, "I'd sure as hell rather double date with you."

The other male chuckled.

"And get my ass handed to me on a plate by the Alpha? No thanks. Besides, I'm waiting for the mating pull. Seems like us simple country wolves like to dream of happily ever after." Nate made a dramatic sigh and batted his eyes.

"Oh, you think it's funny huh?" Clint launched himself at the other wolf and the two immediately began roughhousing. As they continued to banter back and forth.

Cayden laughed and shook his head; he liked these wolves. They seemed like good people, it just sucked that they were in a shitty situation and couldn't find a way out of it. The rumbling crunch behind them made Cayden turn to see the Beta's gleaming red truck pull into the clearing. Clint and Nate jumped up from their wrestling match and dusted themselves off as he climbed from his truck.

"Break time's over boys. Plenty of time for snuggling on your own time." The Beta, a wolf called Russell, called out to them as he approached them.

He had said it with good humour, but it was obvious that they had been rebuked.

"Sorry, Russ. Good to have you here, these pines are beasts; the extra muscle will make this job a piece of cake," Nate replied.

Cayden inwardly cringed. It was probably not a brilliant idea to draw any attention to the fact that the Beta had been slacking in his duties.

Russell's spine straightened slightly, giving him the extra inch or two to be able to look down his nose at his pack members. He stared the other wolf down for a moment before turning his head away disinterestedly, the sun glinting furiously off whatever gel or wax he had put on his swept-back, red hair.

"Change of plan. Alpha needs a job doing. Rose is heading up to see old lady Woods, Alpha wants an opportunity to speak with her alone before she gets there."

"Why? Why can't he just see her when she's working the bar later? Or give her a call?" Nate interrupted, earning a warning look from Russell.

Cayden had been mildly interested in the new orders up until now, it wasn't every day you had to stop logging to play cupid for an Alpha. But the mention of a female that worked at the bar had his ears twitching. Rose. Was that the name of his she-wolf?

*Not my she-wolf.* He tried to remind himself, but his wolf was alert and attentive. His animal did not like the idea of the she-wolf having other males sniffing around.

"Alpha wants to talk to her in person to help her realise what he is offering her. Our job is to stop her and keep her distracted while we ensure that she'll need to pull over further up the track so Sam can come to her rescue."

"I don't like this Russ," Clint spoke up, squaring his shoulders. "What exactly are you expecting us to do, slash her tyres?"

"Not slash them, what kind of a monster do you think our Alpha is? We've just been told to stick them with some nails or something, to let the air out slowly. She won't be in any danger, but she'll have to stop and will need his assistance," Russell replied.

"And what if we refuse?" Clint held the Beta's gaze.

"Then you'd be refusing a direct order from your Alpha and unless you fancy challenging him for the position, you'll be punished for your disobedience," Russell said, the snootiness in his voice told Cayden exactly what kind of a wolf he was. Entitled and felt his position gave him the right to lord it over the other pack members.

"Is that a threat, Beta?" Clint snarled.

"Let's just say it would be a shame if your wage packets went missing for a few weeks." Russell sneered, drawing a deeper growl from Clint who stepped forward with his fists clenched.

*The son-of-a-bitch.*

Cayden snarled, unable to hold back his wolf as it revolted against the scene playing out in front of him.

"This doesn't concern you, wolf. You'd do well to keep your nose out of pack business." Russell snapped at him.

Cayden's inner wolf paced, it's hackles up. It'd be so easy to tear this wolf limb from limb, the pretty boy with his flashy truck probably hadn't won a fight in his life and honestly, he deserved to get his ass kicked.

"Let's not get ourselves worked up over this." Nate chimed in, shouldering his way between Clint and Russell. "Sounds like Sam just wants a chance to act the hero and try to romance the lady a little. We'll do it."

"Glad one of you still has some sense." Russell goaded. "Come on. She'll be passing through any minute. I'll keep her distracted while you boys take care of her tyres." He turned and stomped off in the direction of the main track through the forest. The two pack members followed, shoulders slumped, and brows furrowed.

"Oh, and you can get lost, wolf." The Beta called back to Cayden, "We don't want no outsider thinking he can sling his dick around near our females."

And there it was, clear as day. He shouldn't care. He was an outsider. He shouldn't want anything to do with what was going on with the Darkhills pack. It did not concern him.

But Cayden couldn't deny the fact that he *was* concerned as he marched back to his truck. He saw good wolves being downtrodden by their leaders and kept from bettering their situations. What drove his wolf to the point of madness, however, was the thought that the female who was about to fall into the Alpha's manipulative trap, could be the female that called to him like no other.

Rose. The name suited her. Beautiful and strong. He pictured her in his mind, dark auburn hair that had shone even in the darkness of the evening, green eyes that captivated him, and the call of her wolf; loud and decisive.

The memory of her triggered his wolf's mating instinct. It wanted to hunt her and claim her for its own. The very thing that could never happen. Cayden angrily swung himself up into the cab of his truck and started off up the track that would eventually lead to his trailer. The journey was uncomfortable, and not just because he was tearing up the bumpy track at such a speed that his body was being bounced around behind the wheel. His wolf was clawing at him, snapping angrily, wanting to be let out. He fought to contain himself.

Shifting while behind the wheel of his truck would be suicidal. When he reached his trailer, he stumbled out of the cab, grunting and growling with the effort it took to stop the shift from taking over.

*What the Hell is happening to me?*

He had never had to fight his wolf for dominance like this before. He'd felt desire before, he'd been interested in women in the past, but this burning and guttural need to claim her was overwhelming. Cayden breathed deeply, snarling and huffing as he slowly pushed his wolf back down with an invisible force that caused it to submit. He hated it. It felt wrong to battle with his animal like this, they were entwined souls that lived and fought as one. But finally, he could breathe again, his head was still pounding with the effort it had taken to gain control, but he was no longer about to shift.

Cayden slumped back against his truck. He had no way of knowing that this Rose was *the* she-wolf. She could be just another female. But he kept coming to the same conclusion every time he tried to convince himself that he should stay out of it:

Pack law be damned, he needed to act.

He climbed back up into his truck, he'd meet the main road if he cut back through one of the underused tracks through the forest, and then he'd find the female. It didn't matter if this Rose was *his* she-wolf or not. He would help fix up her tyres and see that she was able to avoid a run-in with the Alpha.

If the wolf wanted to court her, he could do it the honest and proper way. By asking her out and respecting her answer. If Cayden lost his employment for the summer because of this, then so be it.

# CHAPTER FOUR

## *Rose*

Well, that was weird.

Rose put her little jeep back into gear and carried on up the road that led to her grandmother's house.

Russell had gone on and on, asking her about her new apartment and whether he could do anything to fix up the place. She'd laughed when she'd reminded him it was a newly refurbished apartment and didn't even need a lick of paint. He'd kept her there, asking about work at the bar and whether her grandmother needed any errands running. It was sweet of him to offer but she couldn't help but feel like there was an ulterior motive. Rose rolled her eyes. She hoped she didn't have the Beta suddenly sniffing around her like the Alpha was. Russ was nice and all but she had zero interest in him. Her wolf practically ignored him.

Clint and Nate hadn't said much to her and

considering they had been friends since school it had felt weird. She couldn't think what she could've done to have offended them, maybe it was just the heat making them moody. She certainly didn't want to be working under that sun today. She'd take the warm evening air in the forest over the midday sun anytime. She was due a couple days off soon, maybe she'd stay over with her grandma for a night. The two of them could watch trash TV and chew the fat until Gran fell asleep in her chair, then Rose could shift and sprint through the forest, chasing the moon. Maybe she'd see the lone wolf.

A shiver went through her at the thought. He was off limits, but she couldn't deny that she wanted to see him again. Last summer, she had lived for those nights when she'd run with him until they both ran out of breath. Maybe she'd come back after working the bar that evening and spend the rest of the week up in the forest.

*Ah Hell!*

She had that stupid double date. Rose's stomach churned just thinking about being in the Alpha's company and what he would read into it. That's why she was here, she reminded herself. She needed to get some advice from her grandmother. Judy Woods was a no-nonsense kind of a woman who called things as she saw them, but she was also the most kind-hearted and giving person. Her door was always open to members of the pack and she was well-liked, even a little revered by some. Judy had raised Rose as though she were a daughter ever since Rose's parents had passed. If there was anyone who would help her figure out a way of staying within the pack while avoiding the advances of the Alpha, it was Grandma.

Either that or Rose would have to leave.

Lost in her thoughts, Rose hadn't noticed that the ground had started to become more and more difficult to navigate. She had driven this road a million times and her old jeep had never had any problem with the rough surface. She frowned as she realized it felt like she was driving a tank. She continued for another quarter mile before the bumps and jolts became too much. She pulled over to the side of the single track and killed the engine.

Rose climbed out of the jeep and walked around it, looking for any sign of trouble. Her grandfather had insisted before she got her license that she knew enough about a car to be able to maintain it and fix any easy problems herself. He had said it would save her money on the little jobs and help her know when she needed a mechanic, or if she was being ripped off. She certainly didn't need a mechanic now to see that her tyres were flat. All of them.

Suspicion flared in her mind. She'd had the odd

flat tyre before but never all of them at once. She knelt to take a closer look at one of them. A rusty-looking nail was embedded in the rubber. She checked each of the others in turn and found the same thing. Her inner wolf growled, and Rose agreed. Someone had deliberately punctured her tyres. When this had happened, and who was responsible; remained unknown, but she'd find out.

She scented the air but all she could smell was the forest around her and the faint lingering scents of Clint, Nate and Russell. That didn't exactly help; her friends had stood around her jeep and chatted to her as she'd made her way up the road, of course, she'd scent them.

With a frustrated huff, she stood and went round to the passenger side. She leaned into the back and felt around for her tyre pump. She'd re-inflate them and get to her grandmother's where she could take another look at them. Her grandfather's tools were all still there, possibly even a spare tyre or two. She'd be able to fix things up enough before getting to a mechanic.

As she got to work on the first tyre, she heard the rumble of another vehicle approaching. She turned to see a beaten-up, old truck she didn't recognise heading down the road towards her. Her inner wolf stood and stretched in response to the unknown presence. As the truck came closer, her wolf let out a whine and Rose had to clutch at her chest as a sudden thrill of excitement coursed through her. The truck pulled to a stop and she locked eyes with *him*. The lone wolf.

*God, he's handsome.*

Dark hair, almost black, piercing amber gaze that held her captive, high cheekbones, straight nose and a dark, slightly unkempt stubble that could almost be considered a beard. Rose wondered how it would feel against her skin, would it be satisfyingly scratchy, or would it tickle?

Her blood began rushing in her veins heating her as she anticipated his scent again. It had taken all her willpower to walk away from him the other evening when she'd first laid eyes on him in his human form. The brutally handsome face staring at her through the windscreen seemed to be warring with the same thoughts as her. They were desperately attracted to one another, but pack law forbid them from acting on their desires. She, as a pack member, would be cast out and every pack in the area would hear of what he had done; he'd be shunned and liable to attack for the rest of his days.

Nothing could happen. If he were a smart wolf he would drive on. If she were a smart she-wolf, she'd forget about him and wouldn't try to find him running in his wolf form by night.

As it turned out, he wasn't smart.

The man climbed out of his truck stiffly and stood for a moment, closing his eyes as his nostrils flared. He was scenting her. She loved that he was, and a sadistic part of her got a thrill out of seeing the way his broad shoulders and arms flexed as he fought his reaction to her scent. She took small shallow breaths through her mouth. She didn't trust herself not to act on the enticing, woodsy scent of the impressive male in front of her.

The man's eyes darkened with determination as he strode towards her. Rose straightened her spine as he approached, watching the way his body moved. Arousal flooded her at the thought of how his hard body would feel against hers. His nostrils flared again, and a low growl rumbled from his throat. Her wolf practically purred in response. Rose cursed herself for her reaction and for her apparent inability to control it.

He halted directly in front of her, his big frame taking up so much space she had no option but to look up into his amber eyes and breathe in his musky, masculine scent. A growl of her own crept out of her mouth. Rose blushed and bit her lip to stop from going any further.

"Do you need any assistance?" The deep baritone melted over her.

He was just there to help, that was all. He wasn't going to put his livelihood at risk for the sake of some pack female he had an attraction to. Rose chastised herself and tried to rein in her libido.

"I'm good thanks," she muttered, trying to move past him. She needed space. "I've got it covered."

He grunted in response, moving in closer, preventing her escape. She could practically feel the heat rising from him and instead of feeling intimidated, the desire to leap onto him and crush her mouth to his was dangerously powerful.

He leaned in and brought his face alongside hers. The tickle of his beard against her bare skin was torturous and the slow deep inhale he took below her ear caused her to gasp.

*Damn this male, doesn't he know what he's doing is dangerous?*

As if he could hear her thoughts, he pulled back, hands fisted at his sides. She could sense the inner battle going on behind his intense gaze, he knew he was crossing a line but the determination she saw in the way he looked at her, said he had control. An awfully bad part of Rose wanted that control to break.

"You need to be careful; your Alpha is planning something."

That shook her from her lustful haze. She frowned and tried to comprehend what the delicious male had said.

"Sam? What is he planning? Did he have something to do with this?" She gestured to her tyres.

"He wants you and doesn't seem to care about how he pursues you." He growled out, his wolf was clearly not happy with her Alpha and frankly, nor was she.

She knew Sam was manipulative and was turning to underhand tactics to try to press his suit, but she never expected he'd go so far as to tamper with her car, forcing her to break down in the forest.

"And what? He was going to come to my rescue?" She bit out, furious at the Alpha.

The lone wolf nodded grimly.

"Well, too bad for him, I can rescue myself." Rose crouched down and got to work on the next wheel.

Fury coursed through her, dousing the desire she had been feeling a moment ago. She'd be cancelling that double date, Carly and Clint would understand after she explained. She hoped.

"So, I can see," The lone wolf said from behind

her. "It's best that I leave you. But please, be careful."

"I will, thank you for warning me," Rose replied, grateful that he had risked what he had to make contact and help her.

If Sam thought he could threaten and try to coerce her into mating with him, he had another thing coming. A rebellious thought struck her as she heard the lone wolf walk back to his truck.

"Hey," she called after him. "I've missed running with you." At that he turned, his eyes shining brightly.

"Likewise."

"What's your name?"

"Cayden. And yours?"

God, she loved his name. She wanted to say it over and over so she could know how it felt to speak it out loud.

"Rose," she replied, smiling.

She wanted to hear him say her name too. The thought gave her shivers, and her wolf was back to her purring antics.

"Fancy chasing the moon with me tonight, Cayden?" She wasn't surprised that her voice had come out a little husky.

She couldn't resist saying his name and it had felt just as bold and empowering as she thought it might.

A small sigh escaped his lips and his eyes closed. When he opened them again, they were full of trouble, a breathtaking smile lit up his features and her legs suddenly felt like jelly.

"I'll chase the moon with you, Rose, until the sun forces it from the sky and our bodies are weak." His voice was a toe-curling rumble of promise, causing ripples of delight to course through her.

The strength of his inner wolf had rubbed against her own and the effect was an immediate warm and coaxing call to do as he suggested. Her wolf had instantly become submissive and pliant to his influence and Rose had to admit, it felt heavenly.

Feeling hazy, she watched as Cayden climbed back into his truck with a troubled frown and sped away, back up the way he came. He was clearly a powerful wolf to have the ability to press his will unto others, it wasn't a common gift. Even more uncommon that he had used his influence so gently and persuasively. Usually, it was used by an Alpha or Beta to aggressively force submission unto unruly pack members.

With a little distance between them, Rose

grinned after him while her inner wolf shook out its relaxed muscles and began prancing about like a young cub. She had a date. A hot one at that. Sam could go to hell. If he thought he was going to be the male in her life then he could think again. With that thought in mind, she set to work with the rest of her tyres and climbed back into her jeep.

Her grandmother was waiting on her and she sure as hell needed a cool drink and some good advice.

# CHAPTER FIVE

## *Cayden*

Cayden slammed his hand on the wheel of his truck as he drove back up the forest track.

*What the hell was I thinking?*

He hadn't been thinking that was the problem, his wolf had been doing all the thinking for him.

He wanted the female, craved her like nothing else and somehow all his rational thought and sensibility had left him. He inhaled deeply, remembering the perfect scent of her hot body mixed with a sweet perfume. The look of her auburn hair shining in the sunlight contrasted with her sparkling emerald eyes, the smattering of freckles that danced across her straight nose and high cheekbones and her small but perfectly bowed lips that begged to be kissed. If that wasn't enough, the sound of his name on her tongue had driven him to distraction, he'd never heard a more alluring sound.

He had allowed his desires and instincts to overrule him. He was only grateful that he hadn't touched her soft and inviting body. Those enticing curves wrapped up in the light blue denim that hugged her hips, the black tank top that revealed only the most modest amount of cleavage, her bare lightly tanned arms looked smooth as silk and ended with long and delicate fingers that he wanted to feel gripping at his back, while he did all manner of things to her.

Cayden groaned with pent-up torment and his hands flexed on the steering wheel at just the thought of it. He doubted he would've had the strength to walk away from her if he had gotten any closer. But somehow, he had to face her all over again and try to avoid the temptation. He'd agreed to run with her again tonight. He shouldn't. He should stay far away from the alluring she-wolf. She was a pack female. A pack female that had caught the eye of the Alpha no less. He should pack up his trailer and leave. Put as much distance as he could between himself and the sweetest most dangerous temptation.

But he couldn't. Physically couldn't. The thought of leaving her caused a dull pain to throb in his chest. His wolf was pacing back and forth. It wanted the female. Needed her desperately and it sure as hell wasn't about to roll over and give in.

*Damn it!*

Cayden pummelled the wheel of his defenceless truck once again.

He wasn't supposed to do this. He was supposed to stay away from his pack and any other pack for that matter. He vowed to live his life in peaceful, harmless solitude. That way he wouldn't run the risk of hurting anyone again, of ruining the lives of others and causing years of grief and suffering. He wasn't a good wolf. He wasn't good enough to be around others and he certainly wasn't good enough to deserve a mate. Never a mate as magnificent as Rose. Just thinking her name caused a lightning bolt of need to shoot through him.

He knew what this was. He'd seen the strength of a True Mating bond. His parents had been just as strongly connected; just as drawn to one another to the point of obsession. He also knew the devastation caused when that bond was broken, when one wolf died, leaving the other behind. It was like the hole left in their hearts would cause it to rot and they would slowly lose any shred of love and goodness.

He'd felt the full force of his father's anger, blame and resentment as they had come to terms with the loss of his mother, the Luna of the Greystone pack. It had been Cayden's fault that she'd died.

He had been a curious and determined cub and when he had found a fallen baby bird, he'd set off to return it to its mother up on the mountain's ledge. He had felt so brave and focused as he trudged up the mountain path, completely unaware of his mother following stealthily behind, keeping a watchful eye.

He had made a mistake, however, Cayden had climbed a path that was too steep and had slipped on loose stones, causing more debris to fall. He had been swept aside by his mother's powerful black wolf, while her hind legs had been caught by the tumbling rocks and she'd been carried brutally down the slope. She'd sacrificed herself to save him.

That had been the day of his first shift. Cayden had felt his little, fierce wolf tear out of him to call long and fearful howls down to the pack in the town below. He had scurried down the rocky path and crawled to his mother's side, exhausted. Unable to maintain his wolf form, he'd snuggled his shivering naked body next to his mother's fur only to be yanked away and tossed aside by his Alpha father, as he frantically set about trying to free his mate.

She had died in his father's arms while he continued to try to pull her free from the rocks that had crushed her body, and with her last breath, she had shifted and looked to Cayden to speak her love for him. She didn't have another breath to share that love with her mate.

The loss was devastating for them both. It was said that his father even sought out an ancient creature gifted with immortality to try to raise her soul from death, but it had been impossible, his mother had been too far past the point of death for anything to be done.

From that moment on, Cayden was hated by his father. He had been browbeaten into submission at home, never allowed to look him in the eye, never allowed to speak of his mother or cry for her without being punished. In his father's eyes, Cayden had taken away the one bond that had meant everything to him.

Having now felt the intensity of his wolf's connection to Rose, Cayden had a fresh understanding of the level of pain his father must've experienced.

A True Mating bond wasn't what Cayden wanted. Not if it would eventually turn him into the cruel monster his father had become.

He needed to break away from the she-wolf now before their connection grew any further. He would hitch up his trailer, place a call with the Beta to tell him he had found better-paid work elsewhere and he would hightail it out of the Darkhills territory. Rose would be fine. She was a strong and capable wolf with friends and family around her to help her fend off the advances of the Alpha. She would eventually find a kind mate who would treat her well and give her the supportive home she deserved.

His wolf howled in despair.

No. It was for the best, he argued with himself. Maybe he'd sell his trailer and get an apartment in the city. Far away from the forests and mountains that ran in his veins. Far away from any reminder of the female and any temptation of what he could not allow himself to have.

Suddenly his heart slammed in his chest and a blinding pain struck across his temples. Cayden hit the brakes of his truck hard and skidded to a halt, clutching at his chest and pounding head.

*What the hell?*

A sense of foreboding filled him followed by a feeling of imminent danger. Cayden's wolf barked and snarled in his mind, urging him into action. Quickly he swung his truck around sending up a plume of dust in his wake as fear and urgency bombarded him.

Rose was in danger.

# CHAPTER SIX

*Rose*

"You listen here, Samuel Wyatt McClaw."

The angry and no-nonsense tone of Judy Woods' voice rang out through the clearing as Rose pulled up to her grandmother's house. She'd braced herself for trouble the moment she'd turned up the drive and seen the bright afternoon sun bouncing off the Alpha's new truck. Hearing her grandmother about to chew him out would usually elicit a wry smile, but considering what the Alpha had been planning, Rose's temper wouldn't allow her to see the funny side.

"I am trying to make this easier for you all. I don't understand why you're being so damned stubborn." Sam cut in over her grandma.

Rose jumped down from her jeep and stormed towards the house. First, he manipulated her into agreeing to a double date, then he tampered with her car and now he had been leaning on her grandma too. Alpha or not, he was about to get firmly put in his place. If her grandmother didn't do it first.

"Stubbornness hasn't got anything to do with this. If the girl ain't interested, that's it. I am not about to try to convince her otherwise."

Her words filled Rose up to the brim with confidence. No matter what, Grandma had her back. Even if it meant saying no to the Alpha.

"And what's going to happen to her when you're gone, huh Judy? You ain't gonna be around forever, and I'll be damned if I'm going to let you stand in my way." Sam snarled and came tearing out of the front door, not bothering to stop the fly screen from swinging back in her face as the small and furious-looking lady followed him out onto the porch.

Her dark expression was a stark contrast to the billowy, floral blouse she wore over light, khaki pants. Her long silvery hair was swept back from her face revealing the fury behind her normally mischievous green eyes.

"It's Mrs. Woods to you, and you best be thankful that my mate ain't around no more to hear you talking like this." Judy shoved the fly screen aside unperturbed and hollered at the man as he stormed down the porch steps. "But I'm here Samuel, and I am sticking around for a while longer, so you can keep your paws off her."

"We'll see about that, you decrepit old bitch," Sam growled back at her, turning to face the old lady with a face red with indignation and outrage.

With all his blustering and chest beating Sam hadn't yet noticed that Rose was watching his performance. She had seen and heard quite enough, however, and wasn't about to let anyone talk to her grandmother that way.

"You will show my grandmother the respect she is due Sam, or I will have no problem showing my teeth," Rose growled at him. Her inner wolf was snarling and ready to take over in a heartbeat.

Sam turned at her voice, his angry face shifting to one of surprise only to quickly morph back into one of deep rage.

"You will show your Alpha his due respect and submit- before I force you," He snapped at her, trying to force his will upon her.

The thing was, it had the opposite effect and Rose felt her hackles rising further. She felt his will pushing against hers but unlike with Cayden, her wolf stood firmer and refused to become submissive in the face of his aggression.

"I will *never* submit to you," Rose bit back firmly.

"Rose hon, you get on inside now," Her grandma called as she hurried her way down the porch steps.

"I'm done playing nice Rose," Sam snarled as he lunged and caught her by the wrist in a punishing grip. "You'll submit alright, you'll submit on your fucking knees." He yanked her hard as he dragged her towards his truck, causing her to stumble behind him.

Rose pulled and struggled in his grasp, but the strength of the Alpha was greater than she had anticipated. An agonized cry of pain had them both turning to face her grandmother.

The woman had tried to shift into her wolf form, most likely on instinct to protect her granddaughter and had failed. Her back was bent at an unnatural angle and one balding furred shoulder was protruding through the torn sleeve of her blouse. Her body was too weak to transform and as a result, she was potentially left with multiple fractures.

"Grandma!" Rose cried out and momentarily pulled away from Sam's grip.

The Alpha quickly caught hold of her again and turned his back on the injured elder wolf.

"Let me go, you asshole. She needs help," Rose screamed at him.

"Looks like her time is up, and so is yours," He chuckled sadistically.

"Let go of her."

Her grandmother growled and launched herself at the Alpha, partially shifted claws extended and aimed at his face.

Sam released Rose for a second to back hand the elderly lady with a sickening thwack.

Judy went sprawling into the dirt and Rose threw herself down onto the ground to cover her beloved grandmother with her own body. Her wolf wanted out, it demanded she spill the Alpha's blood for hurting the only family she had, but Rose fought against the she-wolf, more concerned with tending to Judy.

Before she had a chance to do more than sweep her hair away from her face, Rose was yanked backwards. This time the Alpha had her in a vice-like grip, his arm bound around her waist. Rose screamed at the top of her lungs while she kicked at his shins and hit at his arms.

"The more you fight it, Rose, the harder it's gonna be," Sam ground out between snarls as he tried to avoid her kicks and punches.

"I will *never* stop fighting you," She screamed back at him. "You won't get away with this."

"You'll stop fighting alright, or I'll go back and finish off the old woman while you watch," Sam growled at her and slammed his other hand down over her mouth to muffle her screams.

That was the mistake Rose had been waiting for. She called to her inner wolf and felt her canines grow and sharpen. Before Sam had a chance to realize what was happening, Rose bit down on his hand and tasted his hot blood. Sam's howl of agony deafened her, but she refused to release him. He went from trying to stop her from getting away, to shoving at her and desperately attempting to yank his hand free from her mouth. With a furious roar, Sam shoved her to the ground and angrily clasped at the gushing wound.

"You'll pay for that, you scrappy bitch. You ain't the only one with teeth."

Rose scrambled up and planted her feet firmly, preparing herself to shift and fight for her life but just as she was about to launch herself at him, a flash of ebony fur barrelled into the Alpha, sending him rolling through the dirt.

Rose's heart jumped and her wolf let out a joyous howl.

Standing between her and the furious-looking Alpha, was her lone wolf.

Her moment to celebrate didn't last long however, in a blink of an eye Sam shifted and his large, sandy gray wolf charged at Cayden. The two wolves became a blur of snarling teeth and claws as they collided with each other, dust from the hard, dry ground was kicked up and the smell of both wolves' blood hit her nose.

She desperately wanted to swing into the fight and help take down the Alpha. Rose hadn't been raised to let others fight her battles while she watched from the side lines, she was a wolf after all: fighting was part of pack life, but her wolf simply watched on with keen, intelligent eyes. She didn't seem in the least bit concerned.

Rose eyed the two males up as they recovered from a short tousle on the ground and circled each other. Sam's wolf was big and bulky and certainly packed a fair bit of muscle, but he was slower than he had been when he'd taken over the mantle of leadership over ten years ago. Sam's preference for sitting back and enjoying the finer things in life while the rest of the pack shouldered the heavy load, looked as though it had taken its toll on his wolf.

Whereas Cayden's jet-black wolf was not only

huge, but he prowled with intent, every step precise and deadly, every muscle coiled and ready to strike. While he may have looked as though he were matching the Alpha's pace, Rose knew he was lightning fast. The only wolf ever to be able to keep up with her on a run and she was known for being uncatchable.

Rose watched anxiously, her gaze flitting between the two males fighting and her beloved grandma who was lying worryingly still on the ground near the porch steps.

*Go.* Her wolf told her. *The male is more than capable.*

Trusting her wolf's judgment, Rose waited until the two wolves clashed once more before running back to her grandmother's side. Her wolf was right, Cayden could send the Alpha running with his tail between his legs, while she tended to her grandma's wounds.

She skidded down to kneel by Judy's side and quickly swept back the hair from her face. She had a nasty-looking bruise marring her cheek and eye on one side and a deep scrape on the other side. Thankfully, her chest was steadily rising and falling with slow breaths. Through her now ruined blouse, Rose could see that her grandmother's shoulder had returned to its human form, all signs of fur gone, but the collarbone was protruding at a painful angle beneath the skin.

Rose held back a silent sob as she took in the full extent of the damage to her beloved, fierce guardian. She must've known her body was too old and frail to shift. Judy hadn't been in her wolf form since long before her husband had passed. And yet, the sweet and loyal lady had almost killed herself trying to protect her. Rose straightened her spine, filling herself up with some of her grandmother's fortitude.

Now it was her turn to become the guardian. She wouldn't let her grandma die like this, she would get her to a hospital and would do everything in her power to make sure she was back to putting the world to rights and reading her dirty romance books in secret, in no time.

"I've got you Gran, and I ain't going anywhere," Rose vowed as she placed a kiss gently on the old lady's bruised cheek.

A furious growl from behind her caused Rose to spin round in time to see the Alpha lunge at her. His teeth were mere inches away from sinking into her ankle and dragging her away from her grandma when the lone wolf landed squarely on his back and sunk his teeth deep into the Alpha's neck.

The speed and ferocity of the attack made Rose gasp in shock. She was rooted to the spot, her feet now pulled back out of harm's way as she sat in the dirt shielding her grandmother.

It all happened so quickly, she didn't have a chance to look away or regret what happened next. Sam's wolf tried to twist free and escape from the huge maw that held him, but all that did was cause the black wolf's fangs to sink deeper. With a swift shake of the dominant wolf's head, the Alpha's thick neck snapped with a final, pitiful whine.

The heavy panting of the lone wolf was the only sound that filled the eerie silence that followed.

Rose watched dumbfounded as Cayden's wolf slowly backed away from the dead Alpha, watching the prone animal with careful intensity. Violence wasn't anything shocking to her, she knew the way of wolves and had seen many males fight to establish themselves in the pack hierarchy. Hell, she'd been involved in fights with some of the females growing up, but she'd never seen a death dealt out with such certainty. She knew fights to the death happened. Her parents had lost their lives in an Alpha challenge when she had been a cub; she of all people shouldn't be surprised at the turn of events. However, knowing such things happened and watching it unfold right in front of your eyes were two very different things.

Rose expected to feel afraid, destroyed by grief for the life lost or at least experience some inner turmoil. Instead, she felt next to nothing about the death of the Darkhills Alpha.

She frowned at her own lack of emotion. Surely there was something there. She had known the Alpha nearly all her life. She'd looked up to him as a kid, as all young wolves did to their Alpha, then as she'd grown, she'd understood a little more of his character and had disliked the man. Based on the past 24 hours she was certain that dislike had graduated to a level of justified hatred.

Finally, an emotion surfaced; simple relief that he was no longer of this world. As though it was one less thing to have to worry herself with. Not the outpouring of emotion she expected but it was something. Rose could accept that; more would come in time.

The heavy and cloying scent of hot wolf blood rose to greet her nose and she was shocked to find that her animal didn't let out a mourning howl at the loss of its Alpha. Instead, she felt her animal's emotions loud and clear, its approval proclaimed in a howl of celebration.

As if he could hear her, the lone wolf's head tilted upward and let loose a long and powerful answering howl of victory that echoed through the trees surrounding her grandmother's house. The sound sent hot shivers through her and any dread that she would've felt at seeing her pack's Alpha killed in a challenge was chased away. The wolf in front of her had defended her and her family and saved Rose from being made to mate with the Alpha by force. In doing so, the big, bad lone wolf had staked a claim:

Rose was his she-wolf to protect and he would kill all those who threatened her.

# CHAPTER SEVEN

*Cayden*

Cayden watched the female as she steadily rose to her feet and stood firm before him. His wolf was high on his victory and the echoing calls from the she-wolf fed his need to claim his mate.

That was what she was to him. He couldn't deny it any longer. The auburn-haired beauty was his mate. He had tried to fight his attraction to her, tried to convince himself that he still had a chance to run from this impending bond, but it was far too late for that. He had felt her fear and anger from miles away and followed it like a flare in the night sky to return to her side. He hadn't hesitated to shift into his wolf and tear into the clearing in front of the elder wolf's house to protect his mate.

The Alpha had signed his death warrant the moment he had tried to force his mate. Lunging for her with his teeth bared while she cared for the elder wolf had been the nail in the coffin. Cayden sniffed down at the body of the dead wolf and huffed his disgust. A wolf like that was better off dead than in charge of a community of good and honest wolves like those he had come to know. But now the fight was done, a moment of doubt crossed his mind. Would the female despise him for what he had done? He drew his eyes back up to meet with hers.

The hunger and desire he saw in her striking gaze swept all doubts from his mind. His wolf growled low in his mind as he began the transition. He'd get his chance to run with his mate soon enough, but for now, Cayden needed to claim the woman. In less than a moment, Cayden returned to his human form, standing as he shifted. His chest heaved and his body was slick with sweat, dirt and blood from the few minor scratches and cuts he had sustained. Nothing that a hot shower and a night's sleep wouldn't fix, and by the look in his mate's eyes, she didn't seem to care as he strode towards her. His body flexed instinctively as she eyed his every move with unabashed desire.

He could hear her pulse beating like a drum as he closed the distance between them and roughly pulled her into him. Rose all-out moaned as his lips crashed against hers. Hot and fevered, Cayden greedily feasted on her lips making his own hungry and desperate noises as he took her mouth like a man possessed.

His tongue swept possessively into her mouth to stroke and tangle with hers, fighting her for dominance. He threaded his fingers through her silky hair to cradle her head as he plundered her mouth deeper. All his senses zeroed in on his mate and the world around him fell away. There was no way he could walk away from her now. Nothing had ever tasted sweeter than his mate and he felt as though he would never tire of kissing her delicious lips.

Rose kissed him back with an intensity that challenged him in the most exciting way. Her hands grasped at his broad back, pulling him closer still, like she couldn't get close enough. Cayden knew how she felt as he tugged at her lower back pressing himself against her. The greedy moan that escaped her had him wanting to thrust up against her like an over-eager teen. All the while the voice of his wolf echoed in his mind, spurring him on. *Mine.*

"Looks like I skipped to the good part."

The croaky and amused voice of the elder wolf was like a bucket of ice water on their heated desire.

Rose broke the kiss and spun around, thankfully shielding his obvious excitement from the eyes of the elder. Cayden carefully kept his hand on her hip to secure her in place.

"Grandma!"

The old lady stretched her neck to try to peer behind Rose. A wicked smile pulled at her lips.

"My, what big...feet you have." Judy Woods grinned and winked at Rose.

Willing himself to regain control of his desire, Cayden coughed awkwardly while Rose gasped, and he saw a flush of pink rise across the back of her neck.

"Grandma, this is Cayden. Cayden this is Grandma or Judy Woods I should say. Cayden just... well, he just..." Rose stuttered, lost for words.

"Just took care of that no good, abusive, pitiful excuse for an Alpha?" Judy offered. "Yes, yes I can see that. About damn time someone put his sorry ass down. We're much obliged young man."

"I didn't come here to kill your Alpha." Cayden tried to explain in a rough tone, his voice still recovering. Although the thought of the dead Alpha quickly helped him eradicate any obvious signs of his arousal.

"No, no, I didn't think you did. You would've done it sooner this summer or possibly last if that had been your intention," Judy agreed as she struggled to prop herself up against the porch steps. Rose pulled away from his hold and he followed as she rushed to her grandmother's side to support her as she leaned back.

"You came here to protect your mate. Sam was too damn stupid to know he was beaten," The lady stated.

"Mate?" Rose gasped and hushed her Grandmother. "Gran, Cayden is a lone wolf, we've only just met. I think we need to get you to the hospital to get you checked out, you hit your head pretty hard."

"Don't you try to palm me off with that horseshit. My head's working just fine. And you haven't only just met, you think I didn't know who you spent all of the last summer running with?"

Rose's mouth dropped open.

"Think I wouldn't smell a male like that?" Judy gestured to him as he stood with his arms crossed over his chest.

Nudity was part and parcel of being a wolf, and now that he wasn't sporting a serious hard-on, he had nothing to be embarrassed about, especially after having just shifted. Sometimes you were naked in front of an audience, it wasn't a big deal.

"As much as I'm enjoying the view darlin, would you mind putting something on? I'm not sure my poor, weak heart can take much more," Judy asked him, frankly.

Rose's cheeks flamed once again as she subconsciously flicked her gaze his way and caught an eyeful from her vantage point, knelt beside her grandmother.

The lady had a point. The positioning was unfortunate and would soon feel rather compromising if he didn't move away. Cayden glanced down at Rose and caught her eye with as much sincerity as he could muster, he didn't want her to think he had no control over his desires. Stiffly, he nodded before stalking off in the direction of his truck that he'd abandoned some way down the drive.

"Boy's gonna put someone's eye out if he ain't careful with that thing," Judy muttered under her breath, but loud enough for Cayden to still hear. A small smile pulled at the corner of his mouth.

As he approached his truck, he gathered up the torn remnants of his clothes, grateful to see his boots had survived the shift, although they had been strewn in opposite directions. He had spare clothes in his truck. Having been on his own for a while, he always kept a bag in the back with enough for a couple of days. He'd not always had his trailer and many a night had been spent sleeping in the back seat of his truck.

As he pulled on some clean clothes, the voices of the females reached him. His hearing was good enough that he didn't need to crane to hear their conversation.

"Grandma, are you OK? Where does it hurt?" Rose changed the subject quickly.

"I've been better my darling girl and I think it'd be quicker if I were to tell you where it doesn't hurt."

"Oh, Gran. I'm so, so sorry. I had no idea Sam would come up here and harass you. He'd tricked me into going on a double date with him and I needed your advice, I wish I'd come to you sooner, then none of this would've happened," Rose gushed.

Anger rose in Cayden once more and his head turned to look at his mate. She was not at fault here and he would be reminding her of as much just as soon as he got a chance to speak with her alone.

"Now, you listen here Rose Woods, you ain't got a thing to apologize for." Judy lifted Rose's chin, forcing her to keep the old lady's stern gaze. "None of what happened here today was your fault. Sam McClaw was an abusive and manipulative man, and it wasn't the first time he'd come up here trying to get my blessing. If none of this had ever happened, he would still be trying to force you to mate him and your True Mate might not have been pushed to act as he did," Judy explained.

Cayden liked the elder wolf even more. She might have been stern, but she was also full of sense and seemed to have no qualms about making her thoughts known. The only problem was that she was about to tell Rose about their mating bond before he had a chance to come to terms with it himself. Cayden pulled on his boots and climbed up into the cab of his pick-up.

The pack would likely be on its way. The death of the Alpha would carry significant repercussions and Cayden wanted his mate and her grandmother far away when he was put on trial. He would plead guilty and then accept his punishment. Rose didn't deserve to be on the receiving end of any of the blame.

Cayden started up his truck and headed back towards the house. Windows down, he continued to listen in to the females as they talked.

"My True Mate? Grandma, why do you think he's my True Mate?" Rose asked.

"He has been pining for you just as much as you have him. Been running around this old house, scenting for you," Judy said with an amused lilt to her voice. "Besides, he just killed the Alpha to protect you." She looked over Rose's shoulder and nodded her head in the direction of the dead wolf. "Not exactly the actions of a mere friendly hired hand?" Judy raised a knowing eyebrow only to immediately wince in pain. Cayden admired the lady's fighting spirit, but it was time to get her seen by a doctor.

The rumble of Cayden's truck pulling up to the house interrupted their conversation. Freshly dressed, he jumped down from his truck and strode over to the two women.

"We better get you to a hospital, Ma'am," He said firmly. "The rest of the pack will have heard the fight, if not they'll soon smell the blood, they'll be arriving soon. I'd rather you ladies weren't around when that happens."

"Polite and smart too. I'm growing fonder of you by the minute, Cayden, darlin." Judy smiled at him and gestured for him to help her up.

His arms came around her, and he gently scooped the old lady up, careful not to jostle her. She was lighter than he thought. A protectiveness swept over him as he lifted her.

"I'll grab you a bag Grandma and lock up the house. They might want to keep you in overnight." Rose stood and Cayden watched her bound up the steps.

He realized they hadn't said a word to each other,

he had just killed the Alpha and kissed her to the point of madness immediately afterwards, and not said a damn word to her. He cleared his throat awkwardly. Still not knowing what to say to her. He turned away from the house and walked slowly and evenly towards Rose's car, careful not to shift the elder wolf in his arms.

"I'll put you in your granddaughter's jeep, Ma'am and she'll get you taken care of."

"You will do no such thing; my granddaughter just had the fright of her life and is in no fit state to drive. You will take us both in your truck and you'll keep her safe while I'm in the hospital." Judy Woods jabbed him hard in the chest as he carried her, making him grunt in surprise. "Besides, I ain't having you throw yourself at the mercy of the pack and take responsibility for that asshole's death without anyone there to tell it like it happened."

"Ma'am, I understand there are consequences to my actions and I'm not about to run from what I did," Cayden argued back.

"I know you're not running. You're doing what a *real* wolf does. You're putting your family first."

Cayden opened his mouth to argue with the lady some more, only to be cut short.

"Hush now, darlin', and do what needs to be done. You wouldn't want to disappoint your mate, now would you?" Judy's voice was laced with humour.

The thought of disappointing Rose caused a dull ache to form in his gut and something about the smug look on the elder wolf's face told him she knew exactly how he was feeling.

*Oh, this old lady is good.*

Tired of arguing with the injured and surprisingly sassy elder wolf, Cayden carefully placed Judy into the back of his truck and turned to return to the body of the dead Alpha. Not that he deserved it, but Cayden would at least see to it that his body was covered from the sun.

"Leave him now, Cayden darlin'," Judy called out from the backseat. "His spirit is long gone. Just nature among nature now, moving him isn't going to change a thing."

Cayden paused and took a deep breath; the words of wisdom were so similar to what he had been told years ago by a pack member when he'd pitifully sobbed by his mother's side. Painful memories threatened to overwhelm him, but the sound of Rose's voice drew him back to the present.

"Grandma?"

"Over here darlin', we're going in Cayden's truck," Judy called back. "Sure is sweet of him to make sure we're taken care of, don't you think?"

The old woman was crafty. If it weren't for the seriousness of the situation, Cayden would've probably chuckled at her cunning. As it was, the old lady was right; he had a job to do. His mate needed to be made safe. With both women secured and as comfortable as possible in the backseat, Cayden pulled out of the driveway and headed off down the back roads towards the nearest hospital.

# CHAPTER EIGHT

*Rose*

Rose hated the smell of hospitals.

She was all for keeping a clean ship and all, hell, she was teased by the locals for the amount of cleaning fluid she used on the floors at the bar, but hospitals were another level altogether. Her wolf wrinkled her nose in agreement. Too many chemicals, too many fake pine scents trying to camouflage the smell of vomit and blood and other bodily fluids. As she sat in the family waiting room, she reminded herself to breathe through her mouth.

Cayden had driven them to a hospital the next town over from Darkhills territory. He said he knew of a doctor there that was a bear shifter. They'd be able to keep a close eye on her grandma while she was in the hospital, and more importantly, would be able to ensure her paperwork turned out looking normal. Shifters tended to be robust and quick to heal, so rarely went to a hospital unless it was necessary. A woman in her eighties with a broken collar bone and potentially other fractures, fitted into that category.

Grandma had been admitted to a ward for examination over three hours ago and Rose still hadn't been allowed to see her or had any kind of update from the waiting area receptionist. Whenever she'd asked, she had gotten the same answer: sit back down and wait. She hadn't been told quite as directly as that of course, the nurses had smiled pleasantly with kind eyes and used soothing voices, but the message was the same no matter how much it was sugar-coated.

Rose fidgeted while she sat, her legs bouncing furiously. Her wolf paced back and forth in time with her. Cayden had disappeared to try to find something to eat for them but honestly, she got the impression that he just used that as an excuse to avoid talking with her. She got it. It was an awkward situation.

He had killed the man who was attacking her and then given her a kiss that was hotter than sin, only to be interrupted by her flirtatious and teasing grandma. He now had to face the consequences of his actions. They both did. Yup, the fact remained that at some point they had to talk about the seriousness of their situation. She couldn't do that without him there.

A small part of her wondered if he was going to come back at all. Her wolf snorted at that, incredulous at the mere suggestion.

*Fine.*

Maybe she was right. The lone wolf might still be a mystery to her, but he showed up when it counted, and so far, had shown Rose that he knew how to do what was right. Rose shuddered. If Cayden hadn't turned up when he did, things could've been a lot worse.

Rose was no damsel, she would've shifted and tried to fight the Alpha on her own, but though she considered herself to be a strong and fast wolf, the Alpha was bigger and stronger than her. He would've won. The consequences of that still filled her with fear. Without Cayden's actions, she had no doubt in her mind about how far Sam would've gone to secure himself a mate.

If her hero would just come back to the waiting room, she could thank him. Shame burned at her. She hadn't even uttered one word of thanks. He had saved her, and she hadn't even told him she appreciated what he had done. Maybe he was pissed with her, she had caused more than just a little trouble for him.

Her wolf rolled her eyes this time.

*Oh, how nice it must be to know with absolute certainty the character of your mate.* Rose thought back at her wolf with a snap.

If Cayden would just come back already, she would have had a better chance of knowing what he was thinking but until he did, how the hell was she supposed to know?

Her wolf huffed at her.

Annoyed by the internal argument she was having with herself; Rose stood and began to walk the room. She wasn't the only person waiting on news. A few humans sat numbly in their seats, some were quietly crying, and others were restless just like she was. Some had small paper cups filled with coffee. It smelt distractingly bitter. What she wouldn't give for a cup. It would probably taste like dirt but at least it would mask the hospital smell and give her something to do.

As if on cue, Cayden strode back into the waiting room carrying two cups of steaming coffee and a bag of what looked like candy bars. Rose rushed to meet him.

"Oh, thank god you found coffee." She eagerly accepted the cup offered and took her seat once more.

"I didn't know how you liked it, but I figured you'd appreciate the sugar," Cayden said softly.

"Usually, I'm a black coffee kind of gal, but this will do nicely."

Cayden frowned and took hold of her cup and swapped it with his own inky, steaming drink.

"Well, that works out well for me; I prefer mine with cream and sugar." He took a long sip of his drink and sighed.

Rose watched his throat work as he swallowed and felt her belly do a little flip. He caught her looking and offered her an awkward, polite smile. Damn, she wished she could shut off her reaction to him. Now was not the time, or the place.

"Sorry I was gone for so long. I had a couple of things that I needed to take care of." Cayden spoke politely, obviously trying to keep them on the straight and narrow.

"What kind of things?" The question came out before she had a chance to check herself. "Sorry, that's none of my business."

"No, no, it's fine. Just had to make some arrangements is all." Cayden's eyes lifted to glance around the waiting room.

Rose nodded her understanding. It was

advisable not to talk about shifter stuff in front of humans who were blissfully unaware of their existence.

"I assume you haven't heard anything yet?" Cayden asked, shifting the conversation on, reminding Rose of her frustration.

"Nope, nothing yet. I don't understand what's taking so long. She wasn't that bad, unless she was in a lot more pain than she was letting on. She could have internal bleeding or multiple fractures," Rose's voice trembled, taking her by surprise.

This morning her grandma had been happy, and they were planning a nice afternoon visit, but since then, she'd gone from thinking her grandma was dead, to relief that she was alive, to now fearing that she was going to lose her after all.

"Hey now." Cayden threw his arm around her.

His clothes smelt slightly musty but the warmth from his skin was divine. The solid, hard bulk of his body felt like a shield wrapped around her. She hadn't realized how much she just needed to be held.

"Your grandmother doesn't strike me as the kind of lady who gives up easily. They just have to run a lot of checks and tests is all."

Rose nodded silently against his chest. She knew

he was making sense, but until she could see her grandma again, she would worry.

"Do you know, while I was hunting down the coffee machine, I think I overheard some of the nurses saying they'd never met a patient who could chew out an entire medical team while having her blood pressure tested."

Rose snorted at that. Encouraged by her small response, Cayden continued.

"Think they said a whole crew of orderlies had to be called in just to restrain the woman so that they could check her temperature."

Rose chuckled at the image he had conjured up.

"Was that before or after they shot her with the tranq gun?" Rose pitched in.

"After, so I heard. But I'm sure they weren't talking about your grandmother. That sweet lady wouldn't make an ounce of trouble."

Rose lifted her face from his chest and looked up into his lightly teasing smile, his amber eyes shining with kindness.

He really was a good kind of wolf, not the bad and dangerous creature everyone made lone wolves out to be. From what she'd experienced today, the wolves she should be wary of were those within her own pack.

No, Cayden was the kind of wolf who knew right from wrong, the kind that lived by an ingrained code of honour. The kind made for mating. Even if it did mean starting a life away from her pack. For the first time in her life, Rose questioned whether perhaps she'd be better off without them.

Her eyes dipped to his mouth. Memories of their passionate and frantic kiss flooded her, and she wondered if Cayden could be as gentle with his lips as he was with her fragile emotions. The thought made her wet her lips and inch closer. A little hum began to spread through her body, one that she was beginning to recognize was a unique reaction to being with him. Just one small taste wouldn't hurt, and wouldn't cause too much of a scene.

"Rose," Cayden warned huskily as he too seemed unable to resist leaning down to meet her halfway.

"Miss Woods?" The distinctive voice of a female doctor drew Rose out of her momentary warm glow with a jolt.

Within a second, she had jumped out of Cayden's arms and was on her feet.

"Yes, I'm Miss Woods."

The woman stood in the corridor holding a clipboard, long dark curls framed her pretty heart-shaped face and she smiled politely. She was tall and elegantly dressed in a form-fitting tailored dress under her white coat and wore modest but glossy high heels. Rose expected someone wearing scrubs and looking slightly harassed, that's what doctors looked like on TV shows. This woman was more put together than Rose had ever been. She *did* own a pair of high heels, she just never wore them, preferring her kicks or sneakers instead. As Rose approached, the woman held out her hand and delivered a firm and quick handshake.

"Thank you for waiting, I'm Doctor Rivers. Shall we move to a private room?"

The woman's eyes were a deep chocolate brown and shone with compassion. Rose didn't want kindness, she wanted to hear that her grandmother was OK, and a private room sounded like she wasn't going to like what the doctor had to tell her. She firmly planted her feet where she stood in the corridor and refused to be intimidated by the professional woman who, admittedly towered above her.

"I'm good here, thank you. How is my grandma? Is she going to be OK?"

Rose felt rather than heard Cayden step up behind her. His presence sent a rush of warmth and strength through her, boosting her confidence.

"I understand you're anxious Miss Woods but

let me assure you that your grandmother will be just fine, in time." The woman's smile widened, "However, I'd like to discuss your grandmother's injuries in a private space, so if you and Cayden would like to join me, I'll be right in here." The woman gestured to several small cubicles that lined the corridor and turned and strode towards one, her heels leaving clicking echoes as she went.

Clearly, this woman was used to getting her way and admittedly she had made it impossible for Rose not to do as she requested. If she wanted more information about her grandma, she had to follow. There was also the small matter of how Doctor Rivers knew Cayden's name. Curiosity and jealousy rumbled low in Rose's gut.

"How did she know your name? Is this the Doctor you know?" Rose asked Cayden in a hushed tone as they followed in the beautiful woman's wake.

Cayden nodded silently.

Rose didn't like it. She had assumed that the shifter Cayden knew was some kind of older, male, father-figure type of doctor. Not a stunningly beautiful, curvaceous, smart and assertive female shifter in her prime. Her inner wolf growled low. Rose agreed. She didn't know how her mate knew this woman, but she didn't like it one bit.

Rose took a seat opposite the doctor and waited until Cayden closed the door and sat down beside her before speaking.

"So how do you two know each other?" Rose knew the first question she had should have been about her grandmother, but fierce jealousy was building a small fire in her belly.

Dr. Rivers seemed to almost be expecting the question and sat back in her chair, crossing her legs at the ankle. Cayden stiffened beside her and cleared his throat.

"Cayden and I met in a bar a few years back and have been friends since." She smiled at Cayden when she said the word friends. "Why, is that important?" The woman looked back at Rose, her eyes twinkling with some unknown merriment.

"It's not," Cayden replied quickly.

Rose held up her hand to quieten him. "It's important, Dr. Rivers because I would like to understand and know all of my *mate's* acquaintances."

Cayden inhaled sharply and tightened his grip on the chair. Rose could feel his eyes boring into the side of her face, but she was more interested in the woman's reaction.

*Yeah, that's right I said it- he's my mate.*

Her inner wolf nodded its approval. Saying it out loud felt powerful and she wouldn't take it back now even if she could. If Cayden was her True Mate, then any other females needed to know about it.

Dr. Rivers beamed and shook her head as though amused.

"Who am I to argue with that?" She relaxed in her chair and laughed lightly, casting a teasing look at Cayden. "You'll have no issues with me, I only wish you'd say that again so I can watch the big guy squirm."

Rose was taken aback. She expected animosity, not amusement and camaraderie. She turned to look at Cayden. He was definitely battling with something internally.

"Say what again? That Cayden is my mate?"

He stiffened visibly and closed his eyes as if searching for control. What was wrong with him? The rising laughter of the good doctor drew Rose's attention.

"Well, would you look at that? Mr. Tall, Dark and Lonesome has finally woken up to the fact that he's an idiot." The woman smiled and stood to get herself a cup of water from the cooler in the corner of the room. "I have to admit this is better than I thought it would be."

"Cayden, are you OK?" Rose asked in a hushed whisper, a frown marring her brow.

"Oh girl, he'll be fine, it's just that his mating instinct is in the driving seat right now. I'm Samantha by the way," Dr Rivers said over her shoulder as she filled her cup.

"Hi. Rose." Rose quickly introduced herself. "I'm sorry but I don't understand. His mating instinct? He was fine a minute ago."

"Yup, and then you called him your mate in front of others, and forgive me for saying but I can scent that you two haven't consummated your mate bond yet, so your little proclamation just made him go into possessive overdrive. He's feeling the need to secure the bond and mark his territory, so to speak." Samantha explained, returning to her chair with a wry grin lighting up her face. "Don't worry he shouldn't pee on you or anything."

Rose's cheeks flamed. She'd known that males were possessive of their mates, but she hadn't known a reaction like this. Although come to think of it, back when they were just dating Clint had once literally carried Carly out of the bar, caveman style, when a customer had gotten a little flirtatious.

"Are you done?" Cayden gritted out, shooting daggers at the doctor.

"Almost. I just want to try one more thing." Samantha smiled wickedly, "You sure this guy's your mate, Rose? Only, I was actually thinking I know a guy who would love to take you out for dinner."

Rose didn't get the chance to answer. A rough growl filled the room and she soon found herself picked up and planted firmly back down on Cayden's lap, his arms wrapped around her possessively and something hard digging into her ass. The speed of it made her gasp and trying to shift herself more comfortably only seemed to cause more rumblings from the man's chest.

The wild hoots of laughter coming from the doctor soon drowned out the low growls coming from her mate. Though she didn't understand the intensity of his reaction the need to soothe him was powerful. With her hand placed against his chest, over his heavily thumping heart, Rose leaned in and placed a small kiss on his rough cheek.

"I'm here. You have me." She whispered under her breath.

Cayden's hand came up and covered hers over his chest while he nuzzled into her neck to take a deep lungful of her scent. The doctor's laughter kicked up a notch again at the sight, but Rose didn't care. Cayden's pulse was slowing back to a steady rhythm and his hold loosened slightly. He didn't let her go but she figured his lap was as good a seat as any.

"Alright, Samantha, you've had your fun, now will you please do your job?" Cayden growled low, clearly still displeased with his friend's behaviour.

The woman sat up at his remark, looking shamefaced.

"You're right. I'm sorry Rose, that was unprofessional of me." She straightened in her chair and reached out for her clipboard that was sitting on the nearby desk.

"It's OK doc, you've afforded me a much more comfortable seat, so for that I'm grateful." Rose smirked, drawing another small and mischievous smile from the woman.

"So, it would seem."

Cayden coughed his annoyance again.

"What can you tell me about my grandma? You said she would be OK?" Rose asked, the seriousness of the situation dawning again.

"Yes, your delightful grandmother, and I mean that sincerely, will be just fine. We had to reset her collar bone which had begun to heal at a bad angle. Doing so has caused some fresh swelling and bruising, but the bone should heal straight now." Samantha explained. "X-rays did show up multiple smaller fractures along her ribcage which are starting to heal on their own and her skull took quite a knocking resulting in some swelling, but it's within normal parameters so there is nothing to worry about there. For an elder wolf of her age, her healing abilities remain strong." The doctor smiled warmly.

"So, is she good to come home tonight?" Rose asked eagerly, relief flooding her.

"Not quite, sorry." Samantha shook her head slightly, "Although you and I know she will heal just fine thanks to her shifter blood, for the rest of the staff at this hospital she had suffered significant injuries and needs to be kept in for a few more days if not weeks."

Rose's shoulders slumped and Cayden's hands gently began rubbing circles on the small of her back.

"Which leads me to the other complication." Samantha sighed. "The authorities want a report on how she sustained these injuries. Your grandmother has said she took a fall down her porch steps. Now, I'm not the only doctor in this place who can tell the difference between bruises and breaks sustained from a fall and those sustained from being struck."

Rose stiffened. They hadn't agreed on what their

story was going to be. She had just been focused on getting to the hospital and making sure her grandma was OK.

"What are people saying?" Cayden asked cautiously.

"The usual: domestic violence at play." Samantha's eyes took on a sad and haunted look. "Look, I know shifters are more prone to physical outbursts. I'm a bear for heaven's sake, we clash heads just as much if not more than wolves, but I need to know what happened here. I'm not accusing either of you of doing this, but if you can tell me a little of what really happened, I can put something down on the report that ensures the police don't go poking around."

Rose looked at the earnest and compassionate eyes of the doctor and decided to trust her.

"The Alpha of my pack was trying to mate me by force. My grandmother tried to intervene, she partially shifted but couldn't fully transition, and that's what caused the break to her collar bone. The rest, I suspect came from the backhand she got from the Alpha. After that, she hit the ground hard. It was a couple of minutes before I could get to her to check her over."

The truth felt easy to say, but the memories of it caused Rose to shudder. Cayden's arms wrapped more tightly around her, and she sunk into his embrace.

"I see." Samantha nodded seriously. "And do *you* require any medical attention, Rose? Or emotional support?"

Rose shook her head. "I'm fine, thanks to Cayden."

"And just so I know whether additional security is needed on the ward; this Alpha of yours? Is he still a potential threat?" Samantha looked directly at Cayden this time.

"No." He uttered with finality.

"Good." Samantha nodded and stood. "I can file the report to say I've spoken with you and confirmed that your grandmother took a bad fall at her home. But a partial shift at her age?" The woman shook her head in disbelief. "That lady has got more grit than any elder I've known."

Rose climbed off Cayden's lap and stood, pride filling her at the doctor's words.

"Can I see her now?"

Samantha shook her head. "She had to be sedated for us to reset the bone, so she's sleeping now. But you are welcome to come back tomorrow during morning visiting hours. I'll be on shift tonight and will make sure she's taken good care of."

"Thank you, Samantha. I appreciate that, can I give you my number in case I need to come in?" Rose asked.

"Of course, just as long as you don't mind me calling you up again at some point so we can swap stories about this big, bad puppy dog?" Samantha grinned and gestured to Cayden who had stepped up behind Rose once more.

Rose looked over her shoulder and grinned at his frowning face.

"Oh, I'm sure that wouldn't be a problem."

# CHAPTER NINE

## *Cayden*

Cayden was seriously reconsidering his friendship with the bear shifter as he and Rose headed out of the hospital into the warm and muggy evening.

He hated being defenceless against his own animal instincts. Having them pulled like he was some kind of puppet on a string, made him vow to return the favour when the bear's time came to mate. Admittedly, it wasn't all Samantha's fault, Rose had started it by calling him her mate in an obviously possessive display.

His wolf stirred at the thought.

Yes, it had felt impossibly good hearing her say it, but the fierce need to covet and claim that quickly followed had been a strange combination of pleasure and pain. The only thing that helped ground him was Rose's closeness and tender touch.

Being soothed and talked down by such a

delicate hand while his friend laughed on, had done nothing for his ego, what's more, the intensity of his feelings sent him to a dark place; made him think of his father. About the times that his father had violent outbursts on particularly bad days, all because he was denied his mate's touch.

He didn't forgive his father for the way in which he had treated him, but Cayden felt as though his eyes had been opened to what torment he must've felt. Cayden took away his father's mate and now he had to go through the torment of discovering his own True Mate. He couldn't help but wonder if this was all some kind of sick twist of fate, a horrible form of karma to punish him for being responsible for his mother's death.

"So, do you know of a motel near here? I don't want to be too far from Grandma tonight in case she needs me." Rose interrupted his thoughts.

Cayden looked down at his petite little she-wolf. She rubbed at the shadows under her eyes and lightly massaged her temples. She had been through one hell of a tough day. The protective need in him rose once again, urging him to ease her stress.

"I've already booked a room at a hotel in town, that's what I was getting done earlier. I figured you'd want to stay close rather than head back to Darkhills tonight. But if you'd be more comfortable in your own home, I can take you back. I need to meet with your Beta soon, so—"

"I really don't want to be back there tonight. I'm tired, I'm hungry and in need of a shower," Rose interrupted. "And I'm not letting you face Russell and the elders alone. So, a hotel sounds perfect. The pack can wait until tomorrow, I'll give my testimony then. Sam McClaw was crooked in more ways than one and I'm not going to let you be punished while he is held up as the perfect Alpha." Rose strode forward towards where Cayden's truck was parked.

God, he admired her fighting spirit. After everything she had been through, his mate hadn't crumbled, quite the opposite; she'd come back up swinging. He wished he could share her optimism about the outcome of the trial. Then again, she was a pack wolf, she'd always receive fair justice. The same didn't apply to those who went it alone.

As he drove them the short distance to the hotel, his mind was dark with the impending meeting with the Beta. Killing the Alpha would result in severe punishment, although considering the circumstances, with enough evidence or testimonials he may be absolved of his crime. The Beta might even feel especially forgiving, considering he now had the opportunity to rise to Alpha status. From what Cayden knew of Russell, he suspected the wolf didn't have much chance of winning an Alpha challenge the old-fashioned way. However, the issue of his growing relationship with Rose would cause unrest, not just with the Darkhills pack, but with all packs in the area.

Although it could be argued that he had only stepped in to protect the female, he had kissed her, held her, and they continued to be drawn to each other. Hell, he was about to spend the night with her, and despite vowing to himself that he would be the gentleman and sleep on the floor, the pounding need to claim his mate was suffocating him. He had doomed Rose to a lifetime of being shunned by wolf packs everywhere, all because she chose a lone wolf over her pack.

That was, of course, unless he stopped their bond from going any further. If he could somehow fight his mating instinct, overcome it where his father could not, and walk away from her without so much as touching her again, he may be able to convince the Beta and council that she was an innocent bystander. Convince them that he was the bad wolf everyone thought him to be, and he had seen an opportunity to seduce the female and taken it. She had only responded due to being overcome by the haze of pheromones released during his fight with the Alpha.

Painting his mate as some clueless she-wolf

caused bile to rise in his throat, but it might just help her avoid punishment and she could remain in the sheltered bubble of her pack. With the old Alpha gone, she would be safe and could have a chance to find a good and kind mate among her own. Cayden would have to be satisfied with the memory of the few intimate touches they had shared.

He still had tonight and tomorrow with her. He would play the role of attentive mate for a while longer. He'd see to it that his Rose was warm, well fed and comfortable. He'd ensure she slept well and got to visit her grandmother in the hospital in the morning. All being well, he would drive her home and then seek out Russell alone. Then he would face his punishment and leave her.

His wolf howled and clawed at him in outrage.

Rose turned her head sharply in his direction, concern dulling her pretty emerald eyes.

"Is everything alright Cayden? My wolf is uneasy."

Cayden cursed himself. Of course, she would pick up on his wolf's emotions. They were *bonding*, and it was only going to become stronger the longer this continued.

"I'm fine, just a lot on my mind." He answered while trying to quieten his wolf.

"Me too." Rose placed her hand lightly on his thigh and returned her gaze to the road ahead of them.

The touch wasn't sexual, simply reassuring. The strength of his mate flowed into him calming his wolf immediately and Cayden couldn't ignore the warm, happy feeling that formed in his chest. Being with Rose felt like home. It made leaving her all the more difficult. He sighed. There was nothing else for it though, his mate would be protected no matter the cost to him.

# CHAPTER TEN

*Rose*

Rose couldn't remember a time when she'd been more grateful for a hot shower.

The room that Cayden had booked wasn't at the fanciest hotel, but nor was it crawling with cockroaches. Rose wouldn't have cared too much if it had been, she doubted she'd be able to get much sleep, not with her grandmother in the hospital and her future in the pack looking increasingly uncertain.

As the hot water eased her aching limbs, Rose started to wonder whether life outside of the pack would be so bad. She would miss her friends. She would miss the forest and the mountain trails that allowed her to run free in her wolf form. She would miss her grandma unless she came with her, and she would miss the home in which she grew up, but she wouldn't miss her job especially. She could get a bar job almost anywhere; she would probably even get a fairer wage without the Alpha skimming profits. Together, she and Cayden could earn enough to put a roof over their heads and could build their own little pack.

Rose smiled. She had found her mate. Despite everyone saying that lone wolves were bad and dangerous, Cayden was good and kind and more than capable of protecting her. He was also the hottest male she had ever known. She wasn't afraid to admit that a part of her was looking forward to spending the night with him. That was, if he would quit being so standoffish.

As soon as they had arrived at their room, they'd had a quarrel over where he was going to sleep for the night. Cayden had wanted to 'do the honourable thing', as he had called it, and sleep in his truck. Rose had chewed him out for being ridiculous and told him that if he were sleeping in the truck then she would be too. After much huffing and puffing, he had agreed to stay in the room with her and had stormed out to find them some food, refusing to take any of the money she offered. Rose didn't mind what he brought back, she was simply happy that he was going to be staying with her and that she was going to get fed.

Rose stepped out of the shower and wrapped herself up in one of the stiff towels hung up on the rack. She had rinsed her underwear under the faucet earlier and hung it up to dry on the heated rail, she fingered it hopefully, but it was still wet. Looked like she'd be going commando until the morning. She grabbed her clothes and opened the door, releasing a cloud of steam into the small but comfortable hotel room. The crisp white linen on the bed called to her. She couldn't wait to climb under the cool, clean sheets but her stomach rumbled, reminding her she needed to eat first.

She dropped her clothes onto the chair by the bed and her heart sunk at the thought of putting on the dusty and dirty jeans and cami top. She especially didn't want to climb onto or into bed with them on. She snuck a glance over at Cayden's gym bag that he'd left by the door.

He had put on fresh clothes after he had shifted earlier that day, so perhaps he had something she could borrow for the night. Most shifters carried a bag of extra necessities in their cars. Clothes getting ruined due to an impromptu shift was an occupational hazard. Rose had grabbed her purse from her car before leaving her grandmother's house but had absently left her spare clothes in the trunk of her jeep.

Thinking it was better to ask for forgiveness than for permission, Rose trotted quickly over to the bag and peered inside.

*Bingo.*

She pulled out a huge, oversized T-shirt and shook out the creases. It smelt musty like his clothes had earlier. Rose wondered how long the bag had lain undisturbed in the back of his truck. Mustiness and creases aside, it was perfect. She quickly dropped the towel and pulled the shirt over her head, smoothing out the soft material over her body. It swamped her but it was a hell of a lot better than the pile of dirty clothes on the chair. Rose picked up her towel and started rubbing it through her long, wet hair as she walked back towards the misty shower room.

She stood in front of the mirror and smiled at her reflection as she finished towel-drying her hair. She looked a little ridiculous in the faded black shirt, all freckles and small arms and legs, but it was Cayden's, and she liked the feeling of wearing something of his.

The sound of the hotel room door opening had her smile widening. She inhaled deeply at the delicious aroma that met her keen nose. Her mate was back, and he had pizza with him. Rose wasn't sure which she wanted to take a bite out of first.

"Rose, are you decent?" Cayden's voice called out hesitantly.

"Sure am," She answered padding barefoot back into the room. "Well, sort of. I hope you don't mind me borrowing a shirt, my clothes are too dirty to sleep in."

Her wolf chuckled as she watched Cayden's jaw drop as she sauntered over to him. Yes, admittedly she put in a little extra sway into her hips as she went, but it was worth it for the look on his face.

"Ooh pizza, it's like you read my mind," Rose said, playing dumb to his continued wordless gaze.

Rose took the pizza boxes and put them on the small desk next to the window. She could swear she could hear his heart racing and his scent kicked up a notch, going from delicious to downright intoxicating. He sure was one enticing wolf.

She continued to play coy and ignored him when he walked up silently behind her, choosing to fuss over their dinner instead. Flipping open the lid of the first box she hummed her approval.

"Pepperoni, an excellent choice." She picked up a slice and turned to face him.

Cayden watched her with barely contained hunger, his amber eyes burning brightly with desire. It would have been a panty-melting look, had she been wearing any panties. The reminder of how exposed she was beneath his shirt and how easy it would be for him to put his hands on her, caused a wave of arousal to flood her. Cayden's nostrils flared as he scented it. Rose loved seeing him react to her in the same way she did to him and the temptation to provoke him further was too much.

"What's the matter? Not hungry?" She took a bite of the hot slice and let out a quiet moan of enjoyment.

"Not for that," Cayden growled as he crowded her in some more.

Rose backed up until her backside bumped the edge of the desk. Heat pooled low in her stomach as she felt the restrained power of her mate surrounding her.

"You want something else?" She asked, her voice betraying how affected she was by him.

"Rose," Cayden warned. "You know exactly what I want but you have had the worst day possible and I'm trying to treat you with the respect and gentleness you deserve." Cayden closed his eyes and inhaled deeply. "Please, don't make this harder than it already is for me." He opened his eyes again and the look of tortured yearning struck her heart.

"I'm sorry, Cayden." Rose took a deep cleansing breath of her own and tried to ignore the heady scent of their lust in the air. "You're right, today's been insane. Why don't you grab a hot shower and afterwards we can eat and maybe talk a little?"

She turned and closed the pizza box up to try to keep it warm. Cayden's hands came gently over her shoulders and turned her back to face him.

"That sounds good to me. I'm sorry, Rose, I just need to make sure you're taken care of. Please eat, don't wait for me." He cupped her face tenderly and for a moment Rose thought he was going to kiss her, but much to her disappointment he pulled away and headed towards the bathroom.

"I'm sorry for taking your shirt," She called after him, feeling embarrassed and a little ashamed for being so brazen with a man she hardly knew.

He paused by the doorway and looked over his shoulder at her.

"Don't apologize Rose. I don't mind you taking it, truth be told, I love seeing you wearing it." His lips tilted upwards into the softest smile that warmed her like a gentle hug. "Eat up, my Rose, I'll be back out soon."

Cayden closed the door behind him, leaving Rose free to let her own happy smile spread across her face. She liked being *his* Rose.

She finished eating the slice of melting, spicy pizza she had started, too hungry not to but decided to wait until Cayden returned before having any more. This was the first meal she would have with him and she wanted him to actually be there to share the moment. It was one of those silly things that her children or grandchildren might ask her one day. What was the first meal you had with your mate? Although this wasn't a traditional date, she wanted to be able to tell the memory of this night.

Rose quickly licked her fingers clean and rummaged around in the desk drawers until she retrieved a small hair dryer. If he was going to treat her with kindness and consideration, then she should at least show him the same respect. Starting by trying to make herself a little more presentable to help regain her dignity while her mate finished his shower.

A sudden realization struck her as she stared at her blushing cheeks in the mirror. Her hand-washed underwear was currently drying out in the shower room where Cayden was cleaning up.

Mortification began to heat her cheeks even further, that was until she heard the unmistakable growl of frustration from behind the shower room door. A giggle swept through her as she imagined his aggravated face as he shook the small slip of pink, silky material in an angry fist.

Rose quickly switched on the hair dryer before Cayden heard her laughing.

# CHAPTER ELEVEN

## *Cayden*

Damn that woman.

Cayden stared at the tiny pink thong that hung innocently from the heated towel rail. His wolf was literally rolling over at the sight of it. He was practically ready to storm back into the bedroom and tell Rose exactly what he thought about the offending item. That it was sexy as sin and now all he could imagine was what she would look like wearing it.

He heard the hair dryer start up behind the closed door and he let loose another growl, safe in the knowledge that she wouldn't hear the pent-up sexual frustration in his voice.

*Damned seductive she-wolf. Why does she have to be so irresistible?*

As if being all hot and dewy from the shower wasn't enough, she'd claimed one of his shirts and was wearing it like she owned it, when in reality, she owned him. Completely and utterly. Her sweet curves had been hidden beneath the fabric but the tiny, stiff peaks of her breasts had taunted him and her long, slim legs had strutted away from him with such command that he was compelled to follow her like some lost, young cub. He wouldn't have been surprised if he had been drooling.

Cayden cursed himself for being so easily caught off guard. He had a plan. He was going to see her safely to her room, get her some food, make sure she was comfortable and then sleep in his truck. But she'd threatened to join him or sleep on the hood of said truck if he didn't share the room with her.

Then he thought he had mustered enough resolve to return with the pizza and face a night of platonic pleasantries only to be greeted with the most delicious of sights. His mate looked refreshed and happy, striding barefoot towards him wearing his shirt with her damp, red hair hanging in dark tendrils over her shoulders. As if she didn't realise she was every hot-blooded male's fantasy.

Not every male. Only him. She was his fantasy. No other guy could see her like that.

The only problem with that line of thinking was he had every intention of letting her go, so she could be with a male who deserved her. Then, that lucky bastard would get to enjoy that vision of exquisite female beauty.

The thought caused a violent stirring of aggression to swell in his chest. Damn it, his mating instinct was killing him. One minute he wanted nothing but the best for her, the next he wanted to give her the best night of her life for the rest of her life, and then he was ready to rip apart any male who dared even look at her: even those that existed only in his own tormented musings.

Cayden growled again and scrubbed a hand over his tired face, blinking at his drawn-out reflection in the mirror. The scratches he'd received from his fight with the Alpha had nearly all faded but there were a few traces of the other wolf's blood on him still. His eyes dipped downward to see that his hard cock stood proudly to attention, mocking him.

*Fuck this shit.*

He climbed into the shower and turned the water on cold. God, it felt awful, but it helped.

With his back taking the brunt of the icy spray, Cayden was able to summon his rational mind once again. Taking long, deep breaths, he felt his emotions calm. His body was tense as a board but at least he was no longer considering pouncing on Rose like she was his prey. Confident that he'd punished himself enough, he turned the faucet and let warm water sink into his body.

He let out a sigh as he finally relaxed enough to squeeze out some of the complimentary shower gel and hurriedly washed himself all over. He didn't intend on spending any longer than necessary touching his own body, for fear of imaginings of the she-wolf's touch entering his mind.

*What am I going to do?*

How could he avoid her in such a confined space when she simply had to breathe for him to want her? It was physically impossible for him to not crave her closeness and her touch.

Unless… a moment of genius struck him, and Cayden smiled to himself.

He would spend the rest of the night as his wolf. He'd curl up on the floor quite comfortably and he would be able to avoid pawing at her.

Shutting off the water, Cayden stepped out of the shower and grabbed his towel. He deliberately avoided making eye contact with the pretty pink talisman of his mate that hung threateningly on the rail. A swift rub down and he opened the door. He shifted into his wolf, who was mightily unimpressed with the plan, and padded into the hotel room to find Rose sitting cross-legged in the middle of the bed.

Upon seeing him, her mouth dropped open. Even in his wolf form, he could appreciate how beautiful the woman was, her long auburn hair was now dry and a mass of loose waves. Her green eyes lit up with humour after her moment of surprise and a wry smile curved her lips. Cayden didn't like the look of that smile.

"Well, then I guess you don't want any pizza after all," She said with a shrug and climbed off the bed. "All the more for me then. I only wish you'd told me you were going to be in your animal, I wouldn't have waited for you."

Cayden lay down on the floor and watched as she opened the pizza box and took another slice. He was famished and it looked like the ultimate cheesy pie, but he had made his bed now, so he would lie in it. He could go without eating until tomorrow morning. His wolf whimpered at that.

"What's wrong boy? You want this?" Rose sauntered over and dangled the pizza above his head.

His mouth may have salivated a bit, and by a bit, he meant he was drooling.

*Stupid wolf.*

"Maybe I'll let you have some if you'll play nice," Rose cooed at him. He was very much regretting his decision as he watched her take a bite.

"Do you shake paws?" She mocked, her smile widening.

Before Cayden knew what was happening his wolf had sat up and presented his right paw for her.

*Damn it.*

Rose laughed and the sound was magical. She shook his paw lightly and held out the slice for him to take. Cayden was mortified that his wolf had overridden his sense of pride and was now playing the good dog, but he wasn't about to look a gift pizza in the mouth. He gently took the food from her hand and quickly gulped at it. His wolf might prefer straight-up meat, but it seemed he was willing to take one for the team.

"Oh, you are such a good puppy, and everyone said you were so bad," Rose cajoled, her hands furrowing through the fur on his head, scratching behind his ears.

*Oh hell, this was a mistake.*

He might have stopped himself from touching her by being in his wolf form but he sure as hell hadn't stopped her from touching him and right now, he was in seventh heaven. Her hands running through his fur was the most gratifying feeling, his wolf nuzzled into her, rubbing his head against her face while she laughed before it rolled onto his back and pawed at her for more attention. God, he was acting like an idiot, but he seemed unable to stop himself.

"Now that I have your attention, Cayden, I have a proposition for you," Rose soothed while lightly rubbing his wolf's chest. Cayden didn't like the sound of this, but he couldn't get his wolf to fall back in line, not while he was being petted and pampered.

*Fucking traitor.*

"I was looking forward to finding out a little more about you while we talked and had dinner together, and if you'd shift back then I'd really like to do just that," Rose spoke softly but firmly. "But if you are so determined to avoid me, which honestly hurts my feelings, then you can stay in your wolf form and I will continue to eat all of the pizza while I snuggle with you and give you belly rubs, only I'll be naked."

Cayden finally managed to force his wolf to snap to attention. He rolled away from Rose and lay on the floor a short distance away from her. His amber eyes watched her every move like she was the most dangerous creature alive. And truth be told, she was. He sure as hell wouldn't be able to resist shifting back to his human form if she were pressed up against him, running her hands all over him and she was naked. Then they would both be human and pressed against each other... naked.

"It's your choice." She shrugged and stood up gripping the hem of his shirt, ready to lift it up.

With a huff, Cayden turned and paced back to the bathroom. He quickly shifted and looked at his defeated expression in the mirror as he pulled on his jeans.

*Damned smart mate.*

"Satisfied?" Cayden grumbled as he re-joined his her.

"Not in the least, but actually being able to hold a conversation with you is much better, so thank you," Rose answered, already climbing back onto the bed with the pizza boxes in hand.

She sat back against the pillows and patted the mattress next to her.

"Come on, I won't bite. Not yet." Rose grinned victoriously. "I'll save that for when we seal the deal."

Cayden sighed and climbed up next to her, resigning himself to his fate. He was powerless against his mate. She wanted something from him, and she got it. He would please his mate however she wished, for now at least. He took the pizza box that she offered and dug in. An awkward silence stretched between them while they both ate. Something she had said was bothering him.

"I'm sorry for hurting your feelings," He said sullenly, between slices.

"That's OK, I get it, this is all unexpected and new. But although I know that everything in the rule book says we shouldn't be together, I don't get why are you trying to avoid me so much? Why won't you touch me like a mate should? It's obvious that you feel the pull between us," Rose asked, keeping her eyes on the pizza in front of her, refusing to meet his gaze.

Cayden supposed it was her way of trying to make a very heavy and loaded question seem lighter. He sighed heavily.

"I'm not avoiding you, Rose." He tried to deny it.

"Uh-huh, sure. You just came out of the bathroom in your wolf form just because you felt like shedding all over the floor."

Cayden laughed at that.

"OK, so maybe that wasn't my smartest move. I'm just trying to be a gentleman here; a lot has happened today, and you should be taking it easy. A lusty wolf sniffing around you is the last thing you need."

"And when did you become an expert in what I

need?" Rose challenged.

She dropped her final slice of pizza back into the box and finally turned her body to face him.

"I never said I was an expert, but I'd be pretty selfish and insensitive to pursue anything the same day that you and your grandmother were attacked. You were almost *raped* Rose and you witnessed me kill your Alpha." Cayden argued back, glaring into her flaming green eyes.

If arguing with his mate was what it would take to keep her at bay, then so be it.

Rose growled at him.

"You *saved* me and my grandmother." She bit out, glowering at him. "And trust me if you hadn't turned up when you did, I would've shifted and fought for my life regardless of him being the Alpha, so I feel zero remorse at the death of that man."

"And if he had forced his influence onto you? Forced your submission?" Cayden countered.

"He tried: he failed. Turns out while he might have been Alpha of the Darkhills pack he wasn't *my* Alpha," Rose replied.

Cayden's mouth went dry. She didn't cower to Sam, but she had easily and willingly submitted to his influence. Her wolf had rolled over and practically batted its eyes at him. Yet another reminder of their bond.

"So, you are an Alpha female. I suspected as much; no wonder Sam was so hung up on you. How come you aren't leading the pack?" Cayden asked.

"I'm not an Alpha. I'm strong but not an Alpha." Rose sighed and looked down at her lap. "My parents were the Alpha and Luna of the Red Rock pack; I was three when they lost a challenge and paid with their lives. I only survived because I was accepted into the Darkhills. I can't be the pack's Alpha. I'm only there through the blood tie from my mother and grandparents. I was supposed to mate when I came of age to secure my place within the pack. When I didn't meet a male I bonded with, I remained within the pack out of courtesy to my grandparents." Rose stood and carried the empty pizza boxes back to the desk. "My grandfather died last summer. It hit me hard. He really was the best, most honourable wolf I've ever known." She sniffed.

Cayden didn't need her to say anymore. The only thing keeping her connected to her pack was her grandmother, who was currently in the hospital. She was being pressured to mate or she'd be forced to leave. Cayden's wolf growled. He was even gladder that he had killed the bastard Alpha.

"I'm sorry, Rose. I... didn't realize you were

under so much pressure. For what it's worth, I don't regret killing that asshole and I'll tell your Beta as much, he needs to know what kind of man was leading your pack."

Rose turned and came back to the bed, crawling to lie on her side.

"They do need to know the truth. Sam wasn't just trying to manipulate me and my grandma, he was also taking a cut from the bar where I work. He was skimming the books of most of the businesses in town to fill his own pockets and increase his status while the rest of us saw our wages cut. I've suspected it for a long time, I was building a case of evidence to bring to the Beta and the elders when Sam upped his game in trying to seduce me. With enough testimonies from others, I'm pretty certain we'll be believed."

Cayden nodded. His female was smart and had been planning on exposing her Alpha to protect her pack. His heart swelled with pride. She was the most admirable female he knew. He might not be worthy of her, but it didn't stop him from wanting to be. He'd help her expose Sam and ensure she could instigate change for her pack.

"A few others in your pack have the same suspicions. I've heard unhappy grumblings about the state of wages and long hours. I think the true character of your Alpha is about to be exposed.

Things will be better for you all once his deceptions are made public."

Cayden turned on his side to face his mate. He couldn't help himself from reaching out to stroke her hair back from her face, revealing the freckles that kissed her cheeks.

*So pretty.*

Rose smiled and leaned into his touch.

"It's the least I can do for them before I leave with you."

Cayden inhaled sharply.

She was killing him with her words. Part of him wanted to tell her now that he would be leaving without her. But a stronger part wanted to savour the moment. He wanted to bask in the warm glow that being beside his mate brought about. He wanted to enjoy one night before she hated him forever, and he ripped apart their mating bond.

"You're a good wolf, Cayden, I never thought I'd find someone who makes me feel so connected. I never knew feelings like this existed, I know it's insane to fall so fast, but I can't ignore how I'm drawn to you." Rose continued, her soft voice like the sweetest music.

Cayden swallowed hard as her hand reached up and stroked his bare chest. Her touch sent ripples of delight through him. He should tell her it was not going to happen, but he knew his emotions were real. He knew the intensity she spoke of and felt how all-consuming the pull between them was. It was only getting stronger. The sexual chemistry was one thing, but he felt such tenderness towards his mate.

She had shared her past without any fear, allowing herself to be vulnerable to him, the trust she put in him was precious and he cherished it. She had proved herself to be smart and brave. She was funny and knew how to tease him, and yeah, he secretly enjoyed it. He admired her and cared for her, beyond anything purely sexual. His mate was the most wonderful person in his world.

"I've never known a woman like you, Rose, you're beautiful in every way possible." His words came out rough and clumsy. Cayden cursed his inability to articulate his thoughts and feelings towards her.

Rose blushed and seemed to gather her courage.

"Cayden, I get that you're being a gentleman and all, and I won't ask for anything else tonight, but please, kiss me goodnight."

Her gentle request was his undoing. He wouldn't deny his mate. He wouldn't deny himself of what he desperately longed for, not tonight.

"You're wrong," His voice rumbled low in his throat as he tugged her across the bed until she was pressed against him, her breath leaving her in a gasp.

"What?"

"You will ask me for a lot of things tonight," He murmured against her neck.

"You will ask me for more. You will tell me to never stop. And you will beg me to make you come. Repeatedly." Cayden grinned at every gasp he elicited as he punctuated his words with hot kisses against her skin. His mate was so responsive to his touch and he wanted to overwhelm her with pleasure.

"And what will your answer be?" Rose said breathlessly as he grazed the sensitive skin at the base of her neck with his teeth.

"A good wolf never denies his mate."

With that, he took her mouth and swallowed her moans.

Tonight, he would enjoy his mate.

Tonight, he would give her memories of him to last a lifetime.

# CHAPTER TWELVE

*Rose*

Rose clutched her mate's chest as he swept his tongue inside her mouth hungrily. God, his kiss was so overwhelming, so demanding and intoxicating. She had feared that her reaction to his kiss before had been fuelled by adrenaline and the strong scent of testosterone in the air, but this was just her and him lying on a hotel bed. The intoxication was purely Cayden.

She massaged her tongue against his, moaning as his hands tightened around her. She had been saved and captured by the Big Bad Wolf and it felt nothing but good.

Cayden's hand gripped her waist and shifted her so that she lay beneath him. He propped himself up to keep his full weight off her and rolled his hips. The hardness beneath his jeans that pressed against her centre made her break their kiss with a cry of need.

"Tell me to stop, Rose and I'll stop. I give you

my word, but otherwise, I'm going to make you cry out like that for me all night." Cayden spoke softly and earnestly against her lips, tugging her swollen bottom lip between his teeth, making her groan.

"Yeah, like that." Cayden moved his lips away from hers and tugged the shirt off over her shoulder and began nipping at her slender neck, making his way fervently down to her collarbone.

Rose squirmed and tried to make sense of the intense arousal flooding her. She felt as though she were drowning in sensation.

"Cayden?" She begged with a ragged voice she barely recognized. "It's too much, please, go gentle, this is too much."

She sighed her relief as he lightened the pressure of his kisses and released his firm hold on her waist.

"Is this better, my Rose?" He looked up at her with amber eyes that shone with tenderness as he softly kissed his way back up to her mouth, every brush of his lips an apology.

She murmured into his mouth as he softly sucked and licked at the seam of her lips.

"I'm sorry, please my love, tell me what you like?" He asked as he continued to gently tease kisses from her.

"I'm not sure, I've not done much more than kiss

before. I was waiting for my mate to come along. I was waiting for you," Rose answered honestly between kisses.

Cayden pulled back and gazed down at her, a look of astonishment in his eyes that soon changed to one of sweet promise.

"Let's see if we can find out what you like then, shall we?" He asked and waited for her to nod in agreement before continuing.

"We already know that frantic isn't your thing," He chuckled lightly and shook his head, a slight colour tinting his cheeks. "Honestly, it isn't usually mine. I'm just a little crazy when it comes to you, my Rose."

She smiled at his honestly and stroked his bottom lip with her thumb. He didn't smile or laugh often she realized, but she loved it when he did.

"I have an idea." Cayden kissed her thumb and gently took her hand in his and began placing featherlight kisses upon each finger. "I'm going to kiss and touch every inch of your beautiful body and when I'm done, I'm going to work my way back up with my tongue."

Rose squirmed under his hot gaze as he let his eyes roam over her.

"Yes, please." She licked at her lips in anticipation and let out a sigh as he began his gentle exploration by kissing a trail along her arm.

When his lips brushed over the shirt, she cursed its existence. His hot breath on her skin was the most exquisite pleasure; to have a dulled version of it making its way across her body had her inner wolf growling its frustration.

Cayden chuckled again and moved his hands down to cup her breasts gently, over her shirt. The action eased her frustration and she found her back bowing to welcome his touch. She hadn't realized how much she wanted to feel him caress her nipples until his hot hands were right there, lightly massaging and teasing the little nubs into stiff peaks through the cotton shirt. She writhed when he flicked his tongue over one. Oh, how she wanted to feel him against her skin.

"Patience," Cayden uttered softly.

Rose wasn't sure if he was talking to her or to himself, but he steadily ran his hands down over her waist and down over her legs. He lifted one foot and gently began rubbing small circles along her instep all the while looking at her with such tenderness and desire that she could've melted right there. Rose sighed happily as she felt all tension leave her and her body became loose and pliant under his careful touch. Cayden smiled at her.

"You like that. Let's see if you like this."

Slowly he placed a single kiss on the sole of her feet before lightly grazing the tender flesh by her ankle with his teeth and chasing away the sensation with a kiss.

Rose gasped when he added his tongue and began slowly inching his way up to the hollow behind her knee. Her heart was beating fast in anticipation as she waited for his next touch, eager for him to go higher. A moan of tortured disappointment slipped past her lips when he started over again with the other foot.

She was both infuriated and delighted with Cayden's soft chuckle as he leisurely made his way up her calf.

"Just think Rose," He teased as he dragged his lips lightly over her skin. "Just imagine how good it's going to feel when I finally put my mouth on you."

Rose squirmed at the thought. The slow, building desire was curling in a tight spiral within her. She clutched at the bed sheets as she willed him to take her further.

With gentle persuasion, he took her hands in

each of his and encouraged her to lift the hem of her shirt with him. Her cheeks flamed at the thought of the slow reveal she was acting out. She paused midway up her thighs. She'd never been naked with a man before and nervousness and self-doubt prodded at her.

*What if I'm not as attractive to him as he is to me?*

The low growl that rumbled from his chest told her that he had picked up on her reservations and disagreed.

He placed more hot kisses over her hands, slowly licking each fingertip while fixing her with a look that spoke of promise and desire. He moaned softly as he leaned in and inhaled deeply at her centre, his eyes closing in ecstasy. Her pulse raced at the sight and, emboldened by his reaction, Rose pulled the shirt up higher and brought it over her head, baring herself to him completely.

Any nerves she felt vanished as she took in the hunger and hot need in her mate's eyes.

"You're so beautiful, Rose," Cayden uttered with reverence as his gaze tracked down over every curve of her body. "My Rose."

He leaned down over her to place a soft and tender kiss on her lips. The sweetness of it took her by surprise. Judging by the look of desire in his eyes she expected another blaze of passion but if anything, this slow and cherishing seduction burned hotter, setting her heart on fire.

Rose wrapped her arms around his shoulders and kept him close to her to prolong their kiss. Their mouths melded together perfectly, each taking their time to explore the other and Rose's hands slid down the broad expanse of Cayden's back to pull him closer. Upon discovering his jeans, she frowned and growled out her frustration.

Cayden pulled back from their kiss and looked down at her with a look of concern.

"If I'm naked, then so should you be," Rose growled, her command drawing a wicked smile from her mate.

"Damn straight." Cayden swiftly kissed her and stood at the end of the bed, he flicked open the top button of his jeans and raised a teasing brow at her.

It was her turn to enjoy a striptease. Rose leaned up on her elbows so she could watch.

Her heart fluttered with every slow pop of a button, her breath catching when he stopped with his jeans slung low on his hips to run his hand up over his chest and back down to dip below the waistband. He watched her wickedly as she wet her lips.

*Goddamn it.*

He was teasing her, touching himself everywhere that she wanted to explore. Her eyes greedily raked over his broad chest, down over the ridges of his sculpted stomach and down past his navel to where his muscles tapered into a delicious V. Every inch of smooth tanned skin looked good enough to eat and her wolf growled, at the prospect of sinking its teeth into his hot flesh, marking him as hers.

"Like what you see, my Rose?" Cayden husked.

Her answer was to launch herself at him. He let loose a full-throated laugh as he caught her in his arms and wrapped her legs around his waist. Her core pressed against his hard stomach felt exhilarating and she unashamedly clawed at his shoulders while rolling her hips against him to gain friction on her aching clit. She cut off his husky laughter by biting down on his lower lip and dragging it between her teeth.

"Stop teasing me, wolf, and give me what I need," She hissed at him, running her tongue down his throat loving the way his breath caught and she felt his chest rumble beneath hers.

"Don't tempt me," He huffed out, tossing her back onto the bed effortlessly. Feeling her mate's easy strength ramped up her need for him and she bounced on the mattress and reached out to slide her hands around to grasp his tight ass beneath his jeans. His muscles flexed and his hand finally slid the denim down.

The impressive length that sprung free made her thighs clench and her mouth water. She had no idea if he would fit but she was damned well going to find out. Her hands left his firm behind and eagerly reached for him. Just as she was about to wrap her hands around his hard thickness her hands were grasped in his as he tutted.

"All in good time." He pulled her up the bed and knelt between her legs. "First, I need to taste you." He pulled her legs wider apart, baring her to his hungry gaze.

She squirmed under his hot scrutiny, desperate for him to settle himself right where she needed him. He leaned down and kissed and sucked at her inner thigh, the sensation causing her to tremble. His hot breath danced over her aching core and she held her breath, waiting for him to close the distance and take her into his mouth.

"Tell me to stop, Rose," Cayden ordered, almost pleadingly.

"Never," She whispered.

With a savage growl, he surged forward and latched his lips over her sensitive bud. Her back bowed and she gripped at the bed sheets as she cried out at the intensely satisfying attack. He released her and began swirling his tongue around her nub making ungodly noises low in his throat. The build of her climax had already begun but when he dipped his tongue down to lap lightly at her entrance, she clenched her thighs against the rising swell.

Cayden growled possessively and pulled her thighs further apart. He licked up her slit with the flat of his tongue to flick her clit lightly over and over before teasingly withdrawing, only to dip his tongue ever so slightly into her entrance. Unable to move her legs against his delicious onslaught, Rose gripped the bed sheets tighter, moaning incoherently as he continued to repeat his demanding torment.

Her climax threatened to crash over her and, sensing her need, Cayden released her thighs to pull her hands away from the bed. He secured them on the back of his head before pinning her hips against the bed with one strong hand. Rose moaned loudly as she gripped his hair and tugged his mouth closer, unashamedly grinding her sex against him.

Cayden suckled her clit hard, his hunger for her a deep rumble in his chest. When he slowly slid a finger into her tight heat, she shattered. Her cry of pleasure ripped through the room as her orgasm struck her like a freight train, a deep and powerful surge of ecstasy that pounded through her, drawn out by her mate's voracious tongue.

"Fuck, I could eat you for days," Cayden cursed as he leisurely lapped at her, giving her body no respite.

The thrumming need built again, and Rose felt her insides tense in anticipation. God, she wanted more of him, wanted to ride the wave again with her mate commanding her body.

"More, Cayden, please god."

He redoubled his efforts and this time thrust two fingers inside of her in a steady pumping rhythm. Rose's eyes rolled back as she groaned and shifted her hips to meet his hand. He was going to kill her, and she would gladly succumb, she thought helplessly as another forceful orgasm broke.

"Fuck yes, oh Cayden, yes," She screamed as she wantonly rode his tongue and hand, lost in blinding pleasure.

Cayden growled against her, greedily licking and sucking at her nub.

Slowly he withdrew his fingers, and her body mourned the loss of him, he stopped kissing her and sat up to gaze at her with lust-filled eyes. She locked eyes with him and embraced the heat that swept over her when he slowly lifted his fingers to his lips and sucked them clean. Her wolf was a dirty boy and it turned her on hugely to witness his raw desire for her.

"So sweet," Cayden hummed his approval and stood from the bed. "With everything that has happened, I don't want you to rush into this. So, I'm going to be taking precautions."

Rose followed him with her eyes as he paced over to where his bag sat on the floor. He crouched down and her body lit up with anticipation as she heard the distinct sound of foil being ripped open. When he returned to the bed fully sheathed, she held out her arms to beckon him closer.

Cayden crawled up the bed, leaving a trail of soft kisses as he reached her breasts. Each of her nipples were already puckered and aching for his touch, smiling into them he kissed and sucked them as he massaged the soft globes gently in his hands.

"My mate is such a feast," He hummed.

Rose moaned as he tugged one of her nipples between his teeth, the slightly painful sting causing an echo of pleasure to resonate on her clit.

"I promised you I would stop if you asked, so please tell me now, Rose, otherwise I'm going to make love to you until you cannot breathe without thinking of me." Cayden lifted his head to pin her with a look of pure need and determination.

Rose pulled his lips down to hers and drew her legs up to tug his hips forward. His thick head nudged against her entrance and the air between them seemed to grow still.

"I need you," She hushed into the quiet space between them.

With slow pressure, Cayden pressed himself into her entrance, his eyes on hers the entire time. The feeling of being stretched warmed her and she longed for him to sink into her all the way. To her surprise, he withdrew slightly only to push in further. The slow friction was the most delicious torture and as he repeated the motion over and over, she felt his body begin to shake with the effort it took to hold himself back.

Seeing his barely restrained need caused Rose's patience to snap. Gripping his shoulders tightly, she locked her legs around the small of his back and tugged him forward sharply. The deep thrust caused a short, hard pinch of pain and Rose gasped as Cayden grunted, his head tilted back, eyes closed in pleasure.

"Are you OK?" His eyes flew open and he looked down at her with the sweetest concern, his breaths ragged.

"I think so, please Cayden, don't stop," Rose

begged.

His eyes darkened and flashed amber with hot need as he slowly pulled almost all the way out, before slamming back into her with gritted teeth.

Rose whimpered at the tight friction that rolled through her. She could already feel her body tensing, demanding release as her mate stretched and heated her with every strong stroke.

"Fuck, Rose," Cayden ground out between pants and he increased his thrusts. "Mine, you are so fucking mine."

He bent down to bury his face against her neck, his teeth grazing the tender spot where her shoulder met her slender neck. She gasped at the contact and arched to give him better access, eager to receive his mating mark.

Cayden tore his lips away with a pained growl and crashed them against hers with desperation. Rose glorified in his possessive actions, pleasure building painfully. As he continued to pump his thick length into her, she lay suspended, on the verge of teetering over the edge of an orgasm that threatened to destroy her.

Sensing her need, Cayden held his weight off her and with one hand reached between them to thrum at her slick nub while sinking deeply into her with long, heavy thrusts. Their hot breaths came in short pants and Rose dug her nails into his shoulders as he pushed her relentlessly towards the edge.

"Give yourself to me," He demanded roughly, pouring his influence into the command, leaving her unable to disobey.

Her climax rolled over her in long pulsing waves that rose and crested over and over, while she called out his name. A roar was torn from his throat as Cayden demanded her pleasure continue to meet his own, slamming into her with hard and punishing thrusts.

"Mine!"

Slowly, his movements calmed and became languid and leisurely. He pressed kisses to her forehead, eyelids, cheeks, nose and mouth, each one a cherishing caress.

Cayden looked down at her with desperate longing while he tried to catch his breath. The emotions held within his gaze caused her heart to squeeze with sadness, her mate was struggling with something. Her need to calm him pushed its way past the receding haze of pleasure, Rose lifted her hand from where she still clutched at his back. She cupped his cheek and smiled, pouring her strength into him.

"Cayden, I'm here. You have me."

He closed his eyes and leaned into her touch before placing a kiss on her palm.

"Beautiful, Rose." He sighed before easing himself off her and padding softly to the bathroom to clean up.

She winced as he moved away. She was a little sore, but happily so.

Cayden returned with a warm, damp towel and pressed it softly against her, the soothing warmth easing the slight sting. She smiled at the tenderness that her mate was showing her after having taken her with such fierce need.

She blushed when she saw the slight pink tinge to the cloth as he took it back into the bathroom, silently. That was her virginity gone. Cayden had tried to go gentle with her but in the end, she had demanded he take her hard, desperate to be connected to him. She beamed at the thought of having commanded such a powerful wolf.

Cayden came back out of the bathroom and smiled softly at her.

"Someone looks pleased with herself."

Rose chuckled and nodded.

"More than just pleased." Rose stretched out her body enjoying the pull on her tired muscles.

"Is that so?" Cayden's lips twitched with amusement as he pulled back the bed sheets and Rose shifted around to do the same.

He climbed in next to her and pulled the covers up around her as she yawned. She wanted to keep talking with her new mate and find out more about him, but the softness of the bed was tempting.

"Well, if you're a good wolf I may just hunt you down again in the night," He husked low, as he drew her to him, so she lay within the safety of his arms. "But first, you need some rest."

"No arguments here," She mumbled as she closed her eyes and snuggled into Cayden's embrace feeling the soft press of his lips to the top of her head.

Rose inhaled deeply, catching the scent of forest pines, and let out a happy sigh. Nothing would ever smell better than her mate. Her wolf agreed and she curled up contentedly to sleep.

# CHAPTER THIRTEEN

## *Cayden*

Cayden watched as his mate slept cuddled up against him. Her soft breaths fanned across his chest like the sweetest lover's caress.

She was the most treasured thing in his world. Tried though he had, she had snuck past his defences and he had been unable to resist her. He had barely avoided becoming fully mated to her, the temptation was so strong during the heat of the moment. But somehow his resolve had prevented him from taking her without protection.

Part of him regretted it. He wished he was in a position to claim her as his mate, but he couldn't give her the future that she deserved. He wasn't the type of wolf that deserved to have a mate to cherish and protect.

Despite knowing she deserved better, deserved a good, honourable, steady wolf from her own pack, he couldn't resist the need to make sure he was her first. He couldn't trust another male to make it worthy of her. He knew that was just an excuse. He was selfish and wanted to be her first, he wanted to know the satisfaction of his mate. He wanted her to always remember who had been the first to satisfy and fill her. He wanted to ruin other men for her.

*Yup, I'm a complete bastard.*

He'd almost given her a mating mark too. He'd felt everything driving him to do it in the moment, his wolf demanding he stake his claim for others to see. How he had torn himself away from her, he didn't know. Even now the need was riding him hard. Cayden lightly swept her auburn hair aside and inspected her neck. It was lightly grazed, and a small pink mark lingered there, taunting him. It would heal he told himself. It wouldn't be visible to her future husband.

Fuck. He hated the thought of another man enjoying her.

His wolf whined and Cayden's arms tightened around Rose as she frowned in her sleep. He told his wolf to quieten down, he wasn't ready for Rose to wake. He needed to get his shit together before that happened. Re-group and form a new plan.

Did the plan need to change? It would be harder now, but he knew that would be the case the moment he kissed her again. He could still see to it that she was returned to her pack. He would give her time to freshen up and settle at her home and then he'd go visit the Beta without her, absolving her of any fault in what happened with the Alpha and between the two of them, and take his punishment.

He'd probably lose his wolf's canines for having slept with her. He didn't care. Rose would be safe, and that was all that mattered to him. His wolf agreed with him on that at least, even if it meant he'd be maimed. They'd grow back. Eventually.

Cayden's phone pinged quietly from across the room. He loathed to leave his mate's side, but he needed a distraction. He slipped from the bed, Rose barely stirred, so deep in sleep. Cayden couldn't help but smile at her soft snores. He pulled the covers up and tucked her in tight.

Picking up his phone he saw a message from a business associate. The man was dangerous, and Cayden didn't always agree with how he chose to conduct business, but he was a good source of income. Sometimes a job needed doing and Cayden knew he could refuse the task if too underhand for his liking. The man also paid his contractors extremely well, to ensure their silence and his privacy.

*Lucian Nightingale: Dear Mr. Greystone, I*

*have need for your services. Respond to arrange a briefing.*

Cayden would've rolled his eyes at the man's ridiculous formality if he wasn't such a scary son-of-a-bitch when he wanted to be.

Cayden considered the message. He would need work now that he'd blown his summer contract with the Darkhills pack, and Lucian's job would likely pay more than what he stood to earn logging timber this summer anyway. It would also be a good distraction for him after leaving Rose behind. It was a no-brainer.

*Cayden: Lord Nightingale, I'm available. What do you need?*

He didn't have to wait long for a response.

*Lucian Nightingale: Excellent. Arrive at Tumbricane tomorrow night. We shall discuss the particulars then. Yours, Lucian Nightingale.*

Cayden sighed.

He hated the mansion where the man lived. It

was dark, foreboding and had a sickly-sweet scent about it. He also didn't like the servants that Lucian kept on hand. They were strange and silent. But work was work, and he needed it. Tomorrow night would be perfect. He might turn up to the mansion a little worse for wear after receiving his punishment from the Darkhills pack, but it gave him somewhere to be, meaning he would have to stick to his plan.

Lord Lucian Nightingale was not a man to be kept waiting.

"Hey handsome, what you doing?"

Cayden lifted his head at the sound of his mate's voice. She was sitting propped up, clutching the bedsheets, her hair was a wild tangle around her head, and she was the most breathtaking beauty that he had ever seen.

"Just taking care of a little business," He replied honestly. "I've been offered some work elsewhere."

"Oh, that's good. Where is it? I can start looking for something too." Rose smiled encouragingly at him, not realizing how her words and cheerful optimism cut him like a knife.

"I'm not sure if I'll take it yet; need to find out more about it," Cayden replied, tossing his phone absently into his bag. His heart ached. He should tell her now that he was leaving her behind. It would be the honourable thing to do, let her hate him. Cayden bowed his head and ran his hands through his hair. He didn't want her to hate him.

"What's wrong? You thinking about facing the Beta?" Rose asked softly.

Cayden scrubbed his hands over his face and looked up into her concerned emerald gaze. He hated to see the frown lines marring her pretty complexion.

"Nah, it'll be what it'll be. I'm going to receive punishment but that isn't anything new." He replied trying to appear unconcerned.

"You get into trouble with packs a lot?" Rose asked, her frown staying firmly in place.

"Not really, but I've taken a few beatings in my time. Besides, it ain't nothing new for packs to hate on a lone wolf."

Cayden tried to brush the impending trial off so that his mate wouldn't worry for him. The less concern and affection she felt for him, the better.

"How long have you been a lone wolf? Have you ever had a pack?" Rose asked, the frown lines fading, her eyes lit with curiosity instead.

Cayden stood and strode to the bed, causing his mate to blush and avert her eyes. She was a sweet female. He thought better of reminding her that she'd become well acquainted with his naked body only a few hours prior. He didn't want to embarrass her.

"Yeah, I had a pack," Cayden answered as he slipped back under the covers and lay back with his hands resting behind his head. "Not many lone wolves are born that way, everybody's got to start somewhere."

"What pack did you belong to?" Rose asked as she turned to lie against his chest. "If you don't mind me asking?"

Cayden looked down his body to where she leaned against his chest. Her warmth sinking into his skin felt like the best kind of comfort and her big, inquisitive eyes gazing up at him were too beguiling to resist.

"I was born into the Greystone pack, but left a few years back after the old Alpha passed," He answered.

Rose's eyes rounded.

"Greystone? Wow! That pack is the stuff of legends. Their territory is huge, and I heard their bloodlines were the oldest and most powerful."

Cayden simply nodded. He found his throat was tight at the mention of his old territory. He loved the wilderness of the mountains and forests where he had been raised. He supposed it was partly why he liked being in the Darkhills. The forested terrain reminded him somewhat of the home that he refused to admit he missed.

"How come you left? Hang on, did you leave or were you banished?" Rose frowned again.

"I left," Cayden replied, satisfied when he saw her eyes lighten again. He didn't want his mate to think he was a criminal.

"So, how come?"

Cayden sighed heavily. He wasn't quite ready to tell her the full truth.

"My relationship with the old Alpha was difficult. When he passed, I left so that there was no shadow hanging over the pack. The new Alpha is a good wolf, and from what I hear, he runs things well."

"I've heard the same. I also heard that the old Alpha was a hard man, lots of wolves feared him." Rose nodded at Cayden's explanation, "Was he really that bad? I mean you said you had a difficult relationship with him and that's why you left, so I guess that's a dumb question."

"He had his reasons for being the way he was," Cayden answered quietly. "But yes, he was hard to live alongside."

Dark memories of his father's violent episodes, followed by hearing the tortured howls of the man's wolf in the night while Cayden had laid in bed nursing his injuries, swarmed his mind. A soft hand cupping his jaw helped draw him back to the present. The memories of the day he lost both his parents ran on fast forward through his mind. He still felt the loss keenly.

"He lost his mate when they were in their prime. She saved her cub from a rockslide but became trapped. The Alpha arrived too late and couldn't save her. Her death drove him insane over the years until he took his own life."

"You seem to know a lot about it," Rose suggested softly, keeping her voice low and steady.

Cayden nodded, staring blindingly at a spot on the wall beyond his mate's head.

"His mate was your mother, wasn't she? You were the cub she saved?" Rose asked.

Cayden stayed silent, willing his emotions to calm. It was in the past. All of it was. Feeling sad about it wouldn't change what happened. It wouldn't erase the years of abuse by his father's hand, and it wouldn't bring his beautiful mother back.

"It wasn't your fault, Cayden," Rose whispered,

her hot tears against his skin shocked him out of his daze.

"It was. If I hadn't been playing on the mountain, she wouldn't have needed to save me. She'd still be alive," Cayden argued. His father's words still echoed in his mind.

*You killed her. It should have been you. It's your fault that she's gone.*

Rose shook her head and grasped Cayden's chin, tugging his face down to hers.

"You were a child. She was doing what any parent would do; protect their cub. You would've done the same had it been your child in danger. I would do the same for our child."

Her words slammed into him and a pained growl tore from his throat.

"Never. Never will you put yourself in danger, Rose."

He quickly flipped their positions and held her securely beneath him. The powerful instinct to protect his mate throbbed in his veins. Her eyes grew wide with shock.

"I would do whatever was needed to protect our child, Cayden," Rose countered, refusing to back down like he wished she would.

Cayden screwed his eyes shut trying to block out her words. He needed to stop thinking about this. He couldn't stand the thought of one day losing his mate, it made him crazy. He could feel the echo of his father's tormented howls resonating in his own heart.

Would Cayden act the same way as his father did? Would he become a violent and abusive monster, lashing out at his own child? He refused to let that happen.

His heart hammered in his chest, and the need to keep his mate safe and the need to run from what he feared would come to pass, warred within him. A pained groan slipped past his lips and he clung to Rose tightly, pressing her into the mattress.

"Hey, Cayden. It's OK. I'm here. I'm safe, you have me," Her voice called to him through the fog of his dark thoughts.

He could feel her calming persuasion pouring through him, she was a strong wolf to be able to reach his soul with her influence. An Alpha female he reminded himself, whether she would admit it or not.

Small kisses peppered his lips, soft and imploring, his mate's body squirming beneath his. Cayden felt his body begin to stir in response. His lips met hers fractionally at first, the soft pressure grounding him in the present. As she licked and nibbled at his bottom lip, Cayden felt a possessive surge rise within him, his mouth opened, and his tongue played with hers in a slow and pleading kiss.

"You have me, Cayden, and I need you," Rose husked, breaking away from their kiss.

Cayden opened his eyes to meet her burning gaze. The delicious scent of his mate was heady and the need to reassure himself of her safety drove him to act.

"Mine," He growled low before sliding down the bed.

He pulled her legs apart and gazed hungrily at her soft and inviting core.

"Yours."

Cayden gripped her thighs and hefted them over his shoulders bringing his mouth right where he needed to be. He licked his lips and with his mate's cries of passion filling up his fragile soul, he feasted upon her until morning.

# CHAPTER FOURTEEN

## *Rose*

Rose woke to the sound of water running. She stretched out her well-worn limbs and rolled into the middle of the bed. Upon opening her eyes, she saw the tangled sheets spread around her and her cheeks warmed with a grin.

Cayden had been insatiable last night, and she'd enjoyed every second of it.

Her satisfied smile didn't last long, however, as she remembered the pain and obvious trauma that her mate carried with him. She sobered quickly. The revelation that her male wasn't just a strong wolf, but the true Alpha of the great Greystone pack, a pack steeped in history and prowess, still had her head in a whirl. He should be leading his pack, but instead, he had abandoned it.

The notion of Cayden abandoning anything didn't sit right with her. She didn't know enough about his reasons for leaving, she had known not to press any further the night before but the wolf she knew, was the kind to do the right thing. He clearly blamed himself for his mother's death and the lasting effect it had on his father, but surely after losing a parent, the closeness and community of the pack would've been even more important to him.

Rose thought about her own formative years. She would've been lost without the Darkhills pack accepting her, each and every one of them was part of her history. Her family.

And yet she was planning on leaving them for a future with her mate, as an outcast.

A shiver of doubt crept into her mind. Could she truly turn her back on Darkhills? Would her grandmother want to give up her home for a life on the road with Rose and Cayden?

Rose sucked in a breath. She knew her grandmother wouldn't want to leave the place and the people that held so many memories for her. The sweet and stalwart lady was laid up in the hospital recovering from multiple fractures, a stark reminder that she was getting on in years. A life on the road wasn't a realistic life for her grandma. The sudden realization that she would be leaving her behind made Rose's heart sink.

Her wolf whined and ducked her head low.

Rose agreed. She had been foolishly blindsided by finding her mate and hadn't thought through the reality of a future with him. Yet she couldn't deny that she wanted a future with him.

Everything in her screamed that her rightful place was by his side like it was her purpose to bring peace to his scarred and tormented soul. He'd sought refuge in her last night as he had struggled with memories of the past. Being able to soothe and heal him resonated deeply within her. It made her feel powerful and honoured to hold his trust. She couldn't imagine being without him now, the old adage seemed to be true, they were two halves to one whole.

Perhaps he would consider joining Darkhills? The thought was a rogue one and considering he had killed the Alpha and seduced a pack female while bearing lone wolf status, meant that he wouldn't be accepted easily by the pack, if at all.

Unless he officially challenged for Alpha. He had killed Sam, so he had more rights than many others to enter the challenge. But considering Cayden had walked away from the mantle of leadership before, she doubted he would want it now. And who in the pack would second his challenge?

Rose sighed heavily. She couldn't see a way past the complications.

Things would work out, they had to. The words of her grandfather came to mind:

*When times are tough, take things one step at a time and you'll find your path through.*

He had been such a sensible wolf, always there for her with words of encouragement and advice. She missed him terribly. What she wouldn't give to climb up on the bench in his workshop and talk with him as he pottered around. While that wasn't possible, she still had her grandmother to confide in, and that was the next step to take.

Rose rolled off the bed and stood, stretching her arms up over her head. She would take a shower and go visit her grandma in the hospital.

Cayden came out of the shower room, a towel wrapped around his middle. Her mate was a magnificent sight to behold. His eyes tracked down over her naked body and heat curled in her belly. The looks he gave were dangerous.

As much as she had no doubt that she would enjoy another tumble with him, she had a game plan to follow. She sashayed past him, pausing to tip-toe up to deliver a quick kiss upon his lips and padded into the steam-filled shower room.

The hungry growl that rumbled behind her made Rose smile. She loved how he reacted to her.

Shaking her head to clear her thoughts she stepped into the shower and got ready to face the day, just as her grandfather had taught her; one step at a time.

# CHAPTER FIFTEEN

## *Cayden*

Cayden shook his head as the shower room door softly clicked shut. Rose was the most beautiful sight. He doubted he would ever stop wanting to lay claim to her. He had needed her last night. The urge to run from the memories of his past and the fear of history repeating itself had been so strong.

The distraction of making love to his mate was like a sanctuary to his soul. She was everything he needed, and all that he ever wanted. But the truth remained that he wasn't good enough for her. He wouldn't condemn her to a miserable and damaging future with him.

Leaving her would likely kill him, or drive him insane like his father, but he'd shoulder that pain on his own. Far away from the woman he would love until his dying breath. It was the only way.

His wolf whined and whimpered at him, but Cayden ignored it. It was time to do the right thing when it came to Rose, rather than being driven by his animal's instincts.

Rubbing absently at the dull ache in his chest, Cayden dropped his towel and shucked on his jeans. He looked at the discarded shirt that Rose had worn the night before and smiled softly at the happy memories that the innocuous material conjured up. He grabbed it up and shoved it back into his gym bag. He'd keep the memento of his mate with him for always.

His phone lit up in his bag, revealing missed messages from Russell.

The Beta was demanding justice.

Cayden knew this would be the case, he was prepared to face his punishment and go through with his plan to absolve Rose of any wrongdoing. What he wasn't prepared for was the video message that showed his trailer burning brightly where he had left it parked within a small clearing in the forest.

Violent flames licked up over the roof, pouring out from the window and door. Heavy breathing and a chuckle could just about be heard over the roar of the fire. As he continued to watch his home be consumed by the blaze the gas canister inside blew and an explosion boomed. A male curse was heard, and the video switched to show a clean pair of worker boots, eating up the ground in retreat before the video cut off.

Cayden swallowed hard and dialled in to listen to the voice message from the Beta.

> *You have something of mine, wolf, and I want it back. See that the female is returned and stay the fuck out of Darkhills. You play nice and we won't hunt you down and kill you. This is my territory now and if you so much as step foot here again, we'll skin you and the female alive.*

Cold fear for Rose slammed into him with a ferocity that seized his heart. He had no choice but to walk away from her now. He couldn't even see her safely home himself before leaving her. The Beta clearly had no qualms about Cayden having killed the Alpha. He just wanted Rose back.

Bile rose in his throat at the thought of what would become of her upon her return. But she'd be alive, and she had a home, a job, friends and family to care for her and protect her as best they could. Which was more than what Cayden could do. He was a strong wolf, but he wouldn't be able to outrun or fight off an entire pack of avenging males. He typed out a quick reply and pressed send, tossing his phone back into his bag with anger.

*Cayden: She'll be at Rivers Hospital by noon. She is unharmed.*

He didn't like it, but his only option was to do what Russell had commanded. For the safety of his mate, he had to let her go.

"Cayden, what's wrong?" Rose rushed from the shower room, a towel haphazardly wrapped around her and threw herself into his embrace. "My wolf is going crazy," She explained, holding him tight.

Cayden wrapped his arms around her and held her back, cherishing the contact.

"Just a little complication with the Beta is all." He swallowed hard, placing a hard kiss on the top of her head to keep her from looking up at him. He couldn't bear for her to see the lies behind his eyes. "I'll drop you at the hospital to visit with your grandma and I'll take care of it quickly before we head back. Nothing to worry about."

"You promise?" Rose stubbornly lifted her head to look at him, her beguiling, green eyes piercing his heart. He fought not to catch his breath.

"I promise, my love," He worked to keep his voice steady.

A small smile lifted at her lips and it was like the

sun breaking across the morning sky.

"My love?" She beamed at him. "I like that."

"That's what you are," Cayden replied honestly. "My beautiful Rose, my love."

His heart broke as he brought his lips down to take hers in a soul-searing kiss. He would remember her like this always. Smiling, contented and warm in his arms. He poured everything into their kiss, wanting to leave her with one lasting memory of the love that her True Mate had for her.

# CHAPTER SIXTEEN

*Rose*

Rose walked through the hospital to the main reception desk with a frown on her face.

Cayden had smiled at her and squeezed her hand tightly as he'd dropped her at the hospital, asking her to pass on his regards to her grandmother. Which all seemed fine on the surface of things. But she couldn't shake the feeling that something wasn't right. Her inner wolf sensed it too, her ears twitching as she lay there, alert. His smile hadn't met his eyes. That was the problem. There was a distance there that she didn't like, it felt foreboding.

Perhaps he was just thinking about what he needed to do before they returned home to face Russell. He'd said it wasn't anything major though. The Beta was probably demanding some kind of payment, with things being as they were in the pack, she wouldn't be surprised if the whole situation was seen as a way of fattening the finances.

Maybe he was thinking about the new business opportunity that he had mentioned the night before. Either way, her mate had much on his mind. It was no wonder really. Rose could sympathize. She too had a lot to think about.

She checked-in and followed the directions given by the kind woman at the reception desk to the ward where her grandmother was recuperating. Rose heard her grandmother's raucous laughter before she even entered the room.

Dr. Samantha Rivers was standing next to her grandmother's bed with a broad smile, her eyes sparkling with humour.

"Oh, Rose my darling girl, come on over. I want you to meet this young woman right here," Judy Woods called, as she beckoned her into the room.

The elderly lady was seemingly in high spirits as she sat up in bed against a pile of neatly stacked pillows. Her hair was loose around her face, but Rose could still see the bruising that painted dark shadows over her skin.

"Hey, Gran." Rose greeted her with a light hug and kiss on her forehead, mindful of her injuries. "How are you feeling today?"

"Oh fine, just fine. I keep telling Dr. Rivers here

that they should let me go already," Judy replied, flapping her hands in the air dismissively.

"Good morning, Rose," Samantha smiled at her from across the hospital bed, "I was just telling your grandmother that she needs to stay in a few more days for observation. But to take the edge off, I've set her the challenge of seeing how many of the male nurses she can make blush before she leaves."

"Grandma," Rose warned cautiously,

"I wager she can embarrass three of them." Samantha smiled indulgently at Judy, her eyes, crinkling at the sides.

"And I told you I'll have 'em *all* turning beetroot before the day is done." Judy wagged her finger.

Rose couldn't help but laugh. Samantha had been as good as her word and had clearly been taking excellent care of her grandmother.

"As if you needed the extra encouragement," She leaned in and placed another kiss on her head.

"If you will excuse me, ladies, I've got a few other patients to check on. But I'll be back later to see how successful you've been, Mrs. Woods." Samantha beamed and glided effortlessly around the bed in her heels. Rose really didn't know how she did it.

"You call me Judy now darlin', and just you wait: before the day is done," her grandmother called back at her as she walked towards the door.

"We shall see, Judy, we shall see. Good seeing you again, Rose, we'll catch up later." Samantha shot them another megawatt smile before turning down the corridor.

Rose looked back at her grandma and smiled. Seeing her in good spirits brought a lightness to her heart.

"So, they've been treating you OK?" She asked as she fussed with her grandmother's bed sheets.

"Yup, no complaints here." Her grandma shrugged lightly, wincing as the movement jarred her healing collarbone.

"Oh Gran, careful." Rose instantly began rearranging the pillows to try to ease her discomfort.

"Quit fussing, girl, and catch me up," Judy ordered brusquely.

"Catch you up with what?" Rose asked, ignoring her request and continuing to plump the pillows.

"What went on between you and that big, bad hunk of wolf last night."

Rose blushed furiously.

"I don't know what you mean…Cayden was a

gentleman," Rose stammered.

"Uh-huh." Judy watched Rose from the corner of her eye. "Darlin, I may be old, and I might not be able to shift anymore but there's nothing wrong with my nose."

"Gran!" Rose chastised. Mortification crept over her and threatened to swallow her whole.

"Oh, don't be so prudish, Rose. It's normal for newly mated wolves."

"Well, if you must know we aren't fully mated yet. Like I said, Cayden was a gentleman. We used protection. He didn't want me to make any fast choices considering everything that happened." Rose finally stopped fussing and stood with her arms firmly crossed over her chest.

"Sounds smart," Judy considered. "Was he good to you darling? You feeling alright?"

Her brow creased with gentle concern as she reached out and took Rose's hand in hers. Judy Woods might have been a hard-nosed queen of sass, but she cared deeply about her granddaughter.

Rose smiled softly, despite the embarrassment she felt discussing such things with her grandma.

"Yeah, Gran, he was sweet with me."

That seemed to appease the elder wolf. She gave

Rose's hand a squeeze and let go.

"Well, alright then." The woman looked down at her lap and straightened out the covers before a wicked grin spread across her face. "Although, I didn't ask if he was sweet; I wanted to know if he was good?"

Rose huffed out her exasperation. The woman was incorrigible. She needed to either lay off or read more of those romance novels, Rose wasn't sure which would work best.

"Yes, Grandma, he was good. Very much so. There are no problems with the wolf in that department."

"But there are problems?" Judy sobered and cocked her head at her granddaughter.

Rose sighed. There was no beating around the bush with her.

"Yes. There's a problem."

"Is it about what happened with Sam? That wolf of yours is more than prepared to take whatever punishment they lay at him, if any. That son-of-a-bitch Alpha tried to force you Rose and he struck an elder. Sam signed his own death warrant."

"No, no. It's not about Sam, although I don't think that helps matters," Rose said. "He's a lone wolf Gran, and he's been with me. Both of us will be expected to leave the pack and no other pack will take us in around here. I'd be leaving you behind and I'm not sure I can do that."

Rose threw herself down on her grandmother's lap, to avoid her seeing the tears that had started to fall.

"Oh, darlin' is that all? You are True Mates; pack law has to take that into account. He could join the pack; he'd need to be vouched for and he'd be low ranked but that ain't the end of the world," Judy soothed, her hands stroking over Rose's hair. "Or you leave with him, baby girl, I wouldn't want to be the reason you fought your mating bond."

At that Rose sat up and looked at her grandmother's soft and kind expression.

"I can't leave you, Gran."

"Oh, sure you can. Your mother left, she followed her heart, and I didn't feel an ounce of sadness."

"But Mom and Dad died, Gran. Look where their mating bond led them."

"I am looking, baby girl." Her grandmother smiled gently and cupped Rose's tear-stained cheeks. "I miss her each and every day, but I don't ever wish that your mother hadn't fallen for your father. Their bond was full of love and it led to you."

Rose cried fresh tears at her words.

"Hush now, darlin," Her grandma soothed as she embraced her again, stroking the back of her head. "It'll all work out."

A commotion at the entrance to the room broke through their tender moment. Rose's head snapped up to see Carly come running into the room closely followed by Clint who wore a look of deep concern. A nurse came hurrying in and threw her hands up in the air before spinning on her heel and rushing back out.

"Oh, thank the lord!" Carly exhaled as she rushed over to Rose and pulled her in tightly against her chest.

"Carly? What's going on? How did you know I was here?" Rose asked as she clung to her friend.

"We came as soon as we knew," Carly half sobbed. "Judy, we're going to make that son-of-a-bitch pay for what he's done to you."

"Knew what? About Sam?" Rose finally pushed away from her friend and fixed her with a confused look.

"We got word that you'd been taken by that fucking wolf. That he killed Sam when he tried to stop him from kidnapping you," Clint growled out. "Russ told him to give you up or we'd be coming for him. The coward told us where to find you."

Rose's head spun with the misinformation.

"Oh Rose, what did he do to you?" Carly pulled her in for another choking hug.

"Now, hold on a second," The stern voice of her grandmother cut in.

"Don't worry, Mrs. Woods, we're still going to track him down. The wolf can't run forever." Clint held up a hand.

"You ain't gonna track down shit, Clint Davidson," Her grandmother growled.

Rose pulled away from her friend forcibly.

"You've got it all wrong. Cayden didn't kidnap me, he didn't hurt Gran, and he sure as hell would never do anything to me that I didn't want him to." Her wolf's hackles raised up defensively and her need to protect her mate pulsed in her veins.

"Oh honey, he did that Stockholm thing on you." Carly's face filled with sadness and pity.

Rose growled her frustration.

"It's Stockholm Syndrome and no I am not suffering from it. Sam tried to force me to mate with him. Sam hit Gran. If Cayden hadn't shown up when he did, I would've most likely been raped by that son-of-a-bitch."

"Are you sure?" Carly asked, her face pale.

"Of course she's sure!" Her grandmother snapped. "Sam McClaw came to my home to try to persuade me to hand Rose over to him. I refused and when Rose arrived, he showed his true colours. He grabbed at her and made it perfectly clear what he intended to do. When I tried to stop him, that bastard hit me and dragged my darlin girl across the dirt."

Her grandmother's witness statement hung in the air between them for a moment. The faces of the two other wolves shifted from disbelief to fury as they absorbed her words.

"Cayden Greystone *saved* me," Rose said clearly, her wolf standing proud. "He is a good and decent wolf, and you can hear it from him just as soon as he gets back."

"Oh god, Rose, I'm so sorry," Carly sobbed again. "I had no idea. Russell told us—"

"Russell told us he'd found Sam's body and that you and your grandmother had been taken. Everyone thought Cayden was to blame," Clint offered, rubbing apologetically at the back of his neck. "I should've known."

"It's OK, how could you have?" Rose offered, her

wolf coming down from high alert.

"Oh hell, Rose, I'm so sorry." He shook his head solemnly. "Russ asked us yesterday to let your tires down, so you'd be forced to pull over. Sam wanted to turn up and act all macho to impress you or something. Nate and I didn't want to go along with it, but Russ said it was Alpha's orders."

"You did what?!" It was Carly's turn to growl, her eyes fixed firmly on her mate.

"We had no choice, we hoped that the tires would hold out until you got to your grandma's." Clint held out his hands in surrender. "I'm so sorry, Rose. I should've been stronger. I should've stood up to him."

"Damn right you should have." Carly glared at him.

"What's done is done," Judy Woods spoke up. "Now we all know the truth and can make sure that the rest of the Darkhills pack knows it too."

"That's right," Agreed Rose. "Once Cayden arrives, we can all head back and tell Russell what happened."

At that moment Samantha strode into the already crowded room.

"Alright, there are far too many wolves in my hospital, and I want to know why." Her face was stern, and her hands were planted on her hips. "Rose, do these two need to leave?"

"No, no, it's OK. These are my friends. There was just a little misunderstanding is all. When Cayden arrives, we'll be on our way," Rose explained.

The doctor visibly relaxed.

"OK, good, but you'll need to head on out. Only one visitor at a time to see Mrs. Woods." She sighed and turned on her heel to leave, pausing at the doorway. "Oh and say sorry to Cayden for me. When I heard we had more wolves from your pack I assumed the worst and left him a message telling him to get his ass over here."

At that, Samantha's phone pinged in her pocket, she pulled it out and read the message. Her face paled and she cursed under her breath. She turned and held the phone out to Rose with a worried expression.

Rose's stomach plummeted as she read the text.

*Cayden: Tell Rose I'm sorry.*

Everyone in the room cowered as Rose's wolf howled its agonised despair.

Her mate was gone.

# CHAPTER SEVENTEEN

## *Cayden*

Cayden's head pounded as he sped along the freeway. If the clawing and biting of his inner wolf weren't enough, his head and heart ached more with every mile he put between him and his mate. He finally pulled over at a roadside diner. His phone had been buzzing beside him in the passenger seat almost the whole way. He snatched it up and saw missed calls from Samantha. He expected this might happen. He didn't even listen to the voice message, deleting it immediately. He just typed out a short text in response. Every word of it was like a heavy weight lodging in his gut.

*Cayden: Tell Rose I'm sorry.*

He tossed his phone back onto the seat and slammed the door of his truck shut behind him. He paced the parking lot trying to breathe and ignore the intense pain churning within him.

His wolf was furious and was causing a snarling, barking storm within.

"I know!" Cayden shouted out loud at his own turmoil.

A few customers entering the diner eyed him warily. Yes, there was a reason for him looking like a madman: he was a fucking madman.

Cayden stormed out of the parking lot and out behind the diner where a small meadow was situated. A few humans were milling about, exercising their dogs; giving them a moment to stretch their legs after long journeys in cramped cars. All the animals pricked up their ears at the arrival of the apex predator and went cowering behind their owner's legs. The suspicious and scathing looks from the humans made him feel even worse than he already did.

Cayden cursed. He needed to calm his wolf down.

He strode through the long grass until he reached the far end of the enclosed field, leaning against the fence he closed his eyes and concentrated on his breathing. The fresh scents of the grasses and wildflowers helped ground his wolf. He couldn't shift and run free out into the mountains that loomed in the distance, not in such a densely populated area, but he could allow nature to flood his senses and lull his animal.

With his wolf finally still, Cayden was able to think clearly enough to reason with his animal side.

"I had to do it," Cayden spoke softly under his breath. "They would've killed her if we'd stayed."

His wolf growled at the threat, baring his fangs.

"We couldn't have taken them all on," Cayden tried to speak rationally to his animal. "One on one, hell, even two or three on one; yes, I'm sure we'd have won, but not when a whole pack stands against us. And Rose wouldn't really want to turn her back on Darkhills. She told us herself, they'd taken her in and raised her as their own. They're all she has." Cayden shook his head sadly. "And we'd be a poor substitute."

His animal paced with annoyance. He knew what Cayden said was true. One lone wolf could never provide the security and stability that a lifelong bond to a pack could.

"Besides, you and I both know what happens to True Mates. We vowed never to put ourselves in a position where we could become like him." Cayden stared out at the mountains and fought against the memories of his father. Thinking of him never did him any good.

"We're not made for the kind of life she deserves. We aren't cut out for pack life. We don't even know how to be a good mate."

His wolf huffed.

"The old man was right. We will never be good enough for that kind of life. All we do is fuck things up and hurt people."

*Like we've hurt our mate.* His wolf pitched in bitterly.

"The only way to give her what she needs is to stay away from her," Cayden said firmly.

He knew it was the right thing to do, but it didn't stop his heart from aching.

Cayden pushed away from the fence and turned back in the direction of the diner. He couldn't dwell on how much saying goodbye to his beloved mate had hurt him. It would only hinder him from doing what was right by her. He needed to focus on something else.

Like rebuilding his life.

His home had been destroyed and the small amount of savings he had wouldn't last long if he were living out of motels. He needed employment. Luckily for him, he had an offer on the table. He didn't know what it entailed or whether it would be something he would morally agree with, but he no longer cared.

Cayden climbed back up into the cab of his truck and slammed the door shut behind him. If doing the right thing caused him this much heartache and misery, then maybe he should make putting his mate's needs above his own, the last right thing he did. The job on offer, regardless of what it was, would give him what he needed. Distraction, money and a way of preventing him from ever considering himself worthy of Rose.

He started up the engine and pulled out onto the freeway. It would be quicker if he took the route back through the Darkhills, but that was no longer an option. The long way around it was. He'd still get to Tumbricane before dusk. Lucian Nightingale would have his dirty, old pickup parked outside his stately mansion for a little longer than he would like.

Cayden grinned at that. The prim and proper son-of-a-bitch hated his truck and Cayden took great delight in refusing to upgrade or even wash the damn thing. It was worth it just to see the slight twitch of disdain on the bastard's face.

With his wolf settled in a miserable slump, the journey passed fairly uneventfully. Cayden ignored the vibrations of his phone on the passenger seat. He'd block Samantha's number or get a new phone if he had to, but he couldn't answer her calls. Eventually, the phone stopped buzzing and he could convince himself that Rose had decided she wanted nothing to do with him.

It was for the best.

Thankfully, tiredness meant that Cayden needed to concentrate more on the road than on his thoughts. It was tempting to stop for a break and sleep in his truck like he used to all those years ago, but he wanted to get the meeting with Lucian over with so he could start focusing on the task at hand; pushing any thoughts of his mate out of his mind.

It was late afternoon when he turned off down the lesser-known track that led to the edge of the Tumbricane estate. It was lesser known and lesser taken. More than once Cayden had to stop his truck to clear some fallen debris from the bumpy track. When he eventually pulled up in front of the mansion, he killed the engine and leaned forward in his seat to crane his neck upwards.

Tumbricane was huge and intimidating. Its towering grey walls and dark turrets loomed above him. Even in the daylight, the place gave off an ominous aura. Cayden had often thought it would make the perfect film set for many a scary movie.

Apart from a small rental, there were no other cars parked outside. Cayden knew that the car wasn't Lucian's. If the man didn't like his truck, he certainly wouldn't have approved of the obnoxiously white saloon. Lord Lucian Nightingale was the type of man to drive a classic sports car or have someone else do the driving for him. Cayden assumed it must've belonged to someone else, likely some city dweller. Most people who lived and worked in these hills drove something a little more substantial.

It looked as though Cayden wasn't the only guest that had been invited. He wondered how many others would be arriving. Perhaps the job required more hands than one. Whatever the situation was, he'd find out soon enough. Lucian had said to arrive after dark so until nightfall he would simply close his eyes and try to get some sleep.

Cayden leaned back in his seat and shut his eyes. The many crows that had made the mansion and the surrounding woodlands their home, cawed loudly, making it difficult for him to drift off. Then his phone began to vibrate on the passenger seat again. He glanced over at it warily, expecting to see Samantha's name on the screen, he sat up and accepted the call when he saw it was Lucian calling.

"If you insist on parking that disgrace of a machine in front of my home, you can at least get out of it and come inside," The crisp articulation of a British accent barked at him. "Only homeless people sleep in cars, Mr. Greystone, and this is not a shelter for ruffians."

Cayden chuckled, unable to hide his amusement.

"I'm glad I amuse you. Now, get inside before I see to it that your vehicle is towed."

"Alright, I'm on my way." He hid his smile and was mindful not to roll his eyes.

He was obviously being watched by the elusive man, despite the mansion looking deserted.

"I cannot meet with you now, but you can at least wait in a guest suite. My manservant will escort you."

With that, the call ended. Cayden shook his head ruefully. Lucian was stuck up for sure, but it appeared he was also feeling generous. Either that or the presence of his rusty old truck really did aggravate him that much.

He grabbed his gym bag from the back seat and headed over to the ornate wooden doors of the mansion. They opened before he had a chance to knock.

"His Lordship wishes for you to follow me," A dower-looking man in smart attire said in a low, monosyllabic tone, his eyes downcast.

Cayden's wolf was twitchy. He didn't like this

place one bit.

*Nothing for it my friend, needs must.* Cayden reassured his wolf.

"Lead the way."

The solemn butler walked at a steady pace skirting along the edge of the main room that acted as a type of assembly hall. This was where Cayden usually met with Lucian to discuss business. The room was shrouded in darkness with thick heavy drapes blocking out any light from the large windows that looked out onto the beautifully manicured courtyard beyond. Cayden paused and frowned. He'd seen the courtyard by night on previous visits and couldn't understand why it would be blocked from view now. Perhaps there was maintenance work going on. Maybe that was the job. Although he doubted it.

The dark room was vast with a ceiling that seemed to rise into the sky. The only light came from matching sconces that hung like sentries on either side of a large and ornate chair that sat at the end of a long run of deep claret carpet, at the far end of the room. The long walk that any visitors would have to endure to speak with Lucian while he sat in wait, was most likely designed to be deliberately off-putting. Cayden always felt as though it were more of a throne room than an assembly hall. People didn't come together as equals in this room.

The hierarchy was clearly established.

Above him, the walls were lined with a balustrade and a walkway that ran the length of the hall with ornate doors spaced evenly along. The rooms that lay behind those doors remained a mystery to him. Every time he had visited, they had been closed. He craned his neck upwards to see the same arrangement continued for two more levels.

To describe Tumbricane as a mansion was an understatement, especially when you considered the rest of the building that encircled the main hall and the numerous other large buildings that made up the estate. Not to mention the bridge that crossed the deep chasm between the mountains and the forest that formed the main approach. The place was a fortress.

"This way, Mr. Greystone," The butler called sternly to usher him along down a dark corridor situated in the corner of the room.

Obviously, this wasn't a sightseeing tour.

It was a good thing that he had no problem seeing in the dark, Cayden mused as he followed behind the man as he steadily climbed a musty-smelling, spiral staircase. The sound of their feet scuffing the stone steps was the only thing to be heard. The hard floor soon gave way to the same claret carpet that ran along the length of the balustrade. Cayden glanced over the side and looked down upon the central hall from the first floor. From this height, he could truly take in the emptiness of the place. The butler stopped abruptly outside one of the sets of tall wooden doors, causing Cayden to halt suddenly to avoid ploughing into him.

He opened the door and motioned for Cayden to enter.

"Lord Nightingale will see you later tonight. You will be called when it is time. Until then, please stay within the guest suite."

With that the dower butler turned on his heel and slunk back into the dark corridor, his footsteps echoing as he descended the spiral stairs.

*So creepy.*

Cayden stepped into the dark room and found the light switch on the wall beside the door. A soft glow from the delicate chandelier overhead illuminated the large and luxurious room. Cayden's mouth dropped. The room was a stark contrast to the cold and sparse hall below. The dark wood-cladded room was warm and inviting. A four-poster bed dominated one side of the room, covered in plush, deep green cushions. The bed was turned down with a matching green velvet blanket decorated in ornate gold trim. Cayden doubted he'd ever seen a bigger bed. An empty hearth sat opposite the bed, with two comfortable chesterfield armchairs in dark red leather placed on either side. A low coffee table sat between them, a sparkling crystal decanter and accompanying tumblers perched at the centre. A deep amber liquid shone from within. An extremely thoughtful gesture.

Cayden shut the door behind him and walked in, dropping his bag by the door. He reached for the heavy golden drapes and pulled them back. The room flooded with sunlight, and the perfectly kept courtyard garden below drew his eye. The fountains dotted throughout the meandering paths trickled gently and the colour of the roses below was the most vibrant he had ever seen.

*Rose.*

Thoughts of her sprung to mind and he shut out the image of her delicate features, refusing to pay any notice to the sharp stab to his heart. He closed his eyes and took a deep breath. When he opened them again, he looked out over the gardens with blind eyes.

Definitely not a gardening job required, Cayden mused. He couldn't understand why the view had been blocked from the room below.

As much as he enjoyed the view of the garden, his eyes were heavy, and he doubted he'd have the opportunity again to sleep in such luxurious surroundings. Cayden dragged the curtains shut once more and headed over to the coffee table, he passed a giant free-standing bathtub in one corner, discreetly hidden from the rest of the room by an ornate golden silk screen. He wasn't usually one for taking long baths, but in the absence of a shower perhaps he'd take a dip later. Until then he would ensure he got a good few hours of sleep.

Cayden carried the heavy decanter and one of the tumblers back to the bed and climbed on. The mattress moulded to him and as he sat back against the headboard, taking greedy gulps of the fiery whiskey, he told his mind to switch off.

He wouldn't think of her. He had no right to even dream of her. He was a lone wolf and that was the way he would stay.

He knocked back another glass of the strong liquor, enjoying the burn that scorched down his throat and pooled in his belly. His wolf's eyes shuttered, and he curled up. He placed the decanter and glass on the bedside table and flicked the switch on the wall beside him. The glow of the chandelier gently faded to nothing.

With a heavy heart, Cayden welcomed how the quiet darkness of the room pulled him under. He just hoped the oblivion that would follow would give him the peace he craved.

# CHAPTER EIGHTEEN

## *Rose*

Rose closed her apartment door and slumped down onto her couch. She'd said goodbye to her friends in the car, refusing their offers to come up with her and get her settled back in.

Cayden was gone.

Every part of her ached, from her head down to her toes. Her heart felt like it had been shattered into a thousand pieces and Rose didn't even know if it could ever be put back together again. Her wolf had exhausted herself in her grief and was thankfully still for now. She lay lifelessly, staring out into some invisible, dark abyss.

She'd tried hundreds of times to contact Cayden. Samantha was relentless in her efforts to call him and leave him messages. Rose had taken his number and had called him over and over, had written out dozens of text messages to him. There was no reply.

She'd eventually given up any hope that he would come back, and her grandmother and friends had convinced her to return home. Samantha had promised to continue to take good care of her grandmother and to stay in touch. She wasn't going to give up on trying to get hold of Cayden either.

The journey home had been a long and silent one. Carly had tried to talk with Rose, she'd tried to soothe, tried to ask her about her feelings, tried to instigate her to be angry. But it hadn't worked. Finally, Clint had placed his hand upon Carly's leg and shook his head at her. The quiet that followed was better. She appreciated the support of her friends, but nothing would help her.

Her mate was gone. He had left her.

She wanted to be angry with him. She wanted to be able to hate him, but she just didn't have it within her. She had nothing inside. Just a vast chasm of emptiness where her heart used to be. Somehow, she had loved and lost in less than forty-eight hours.

Rose lay back on the couch staring up at the ceiling. What was there for her now? Hours ago, she had been contemplating how to get the pack to accept Cayden as her mate. This morning she'd been nestled in his arms after the most beautiful night with him and everything had felt so right. The echo of the utter contentment she had felt in that moment haunted her. She wrapped her arms around herself and squeezed tight to try to ease the emptiness. It didn't help.

She would do right by her mate. He may have left but she still knew him to be a good male. She would set the record straight with Russell and the pack. He was an honourable wolf. Despite not returning to face the repercussions of his actions.

Frustration welled within her. It was the one emotion other than her initial despair that she felt.

*Why has he left? Why didn't he return to speak with Russell?*

Russell had contacted him that morning. Cayden said he had to sort some things for the Beta. Had that all been a lie, or was that why he had left? Had Russell demanded it?

Rose shook her head. Russell, despite being Beta and soon to be Alpha, was not a commanding wolf. He was eager to please and was the epitome of the nice, boy next door. Always offering to help, always polite. His over-the-top niceness grated on Rose a little if she were truthful, but he was harmless. She couldn't see Russell ever demanding anything.

As if summoned, there came a knock at her door, followed by the Beta calling out a greeting.

"Rose, you in there? You OK? I just wanted to check on you, wanted to talk. If you feel up to it, that is."

She rolled her eyes and sat up. It was time to face the music. She could at least restore Cayden's reputation, regardless of how he felt about her, she still felt a strong need to protect him. She stood and squared her shoulders and went to open the door.

Russell stood in the hallway clutching an extravagantly large bouquet of flowers. He had taken off his cap and smoothed his burnt orange hair down. Clearly, he was making an effort, but Rose wasn't sure why.

"Oh Rose, you have no idea how good it is to see you again. I've been beside myself worrying for you." He thrust the flowers into her hands. "I got these for you. I know they can't make up for everything that you've been through, but I guess, I don't know. I guess I just wanted you to see how much you're cared for." He fixed her with the biggest puppy dog eyes, which would've been comical had it not been so off-putting and out of place.

"Russell, hi," Rose greeted him in return. "Thank you for thinking of me. They're lovely. But you needn't have worried. I'm fine now, thanks to Cayden."

Best to get straight to it and not draw this out any longer than it needed to be.

"I'm not sure I understand, sweetheart. Can I come in?"

Rose nodded and showed him into her apartment, ushering him to take a seat on the couch. She laid the flowers down on the coffee table and sat beside him. She knew she should probably offer him some refreshments. Her grandmother had taught her proper manners, but honestly, she just wanted this over with so she could go to bed and likely cry herself to sleep.

"Now, how did you manage to escape him?" Russell asked, taking her hands in his own. The action caused a shiver of distaste to roll over her. "Oh sweetheart, look at you; you're shaking. Can I get you anything?" Russell soothed.

It was both ingratiating and frustrating.

"No, I'm fine, Russ. Thank you. And I didn't escape him. He left me and grandma at the hospital. He took her there after she had been hurt by Sam."

"Sam?" Russell's eyes squinted. "Sweetheart, are you sure that wolf didn't hit you on your head?"

"No," Rose said firmly. "Cayden never raised a hand against me or my grandmother. He saved me, Russ. Sam was at my grandmother's house trying to get her to convince me to be his mate. She refused. When I showed up, he just went crazy. He grabbed me and when she tried to stop him, he hit her. Sent her flying." Rose paused, the memory of seeing her beloved grandma go spinning down into the dirt causing her to suck in a breath. "Sam then started dragging me towards his truck, saying that I'd be mated to him one way or another. Cayden showed up just in time and fought Sam off. When he tried to attack me again, Cayden killed him."

Russell sat there with eyes like saucers.

"Are you sure Rose? I cannot believe that Sam would try to force you."

"He did, Russ. He was not a good Alpha. He was an abusive and violent asshole who intended on raping me. My grandmother will tell you the same thing," Rose said, staring him down.

Russell shook his head sadly and stood to pace the room.

"I can't believe it. Well, I believe you, Rose, I do. It's just… it's hard to get my head around."

"Sam wasn't a good wolf before this either, Russ. He'd been stealing profits from the bar and from a handful of other businesses in town too, I was gathering evidence to bring to you, but he was lining his pockets while the rest of the pack struggled to pay the bills." Rose continued; the true character of Sam McClaw needed to be made known.

Russell stopped pacing and held out a hand to halt her.

"Let's just take this one thing at a time, sweetheart."

"Sam's death was deserved, Russ. Pack law dictates that forcing a female is punishable by death. Cayden should be absolved of any wrongdoing. He acted honourably."

"That's another problem, Rose," Russell said his face morphing into one of serious concern as he returned to sit by her side.

"What do you mean?" She frowned.

"He hasn't been honourable. He... how do I put this?" Russell paused and glanced swiftly away at the ground before looking at her with embarrassment. "He has *interfered* with you, hasn't he sweetheart?"

Anger bubbled up from within her.

"I'm not fully mated if that's what you're suggesting," Rose gritted out, trying to ignore the bitterness that came with her words.

"No, no of course not *fully* mated. I can scent that you aren't," Russell rushed out. "However, you have slept with him."

"And why is that your concern?" Rose snapped

"I know. I know, Rose, this is all extremely awkward and trust me, I really wish that I wasn't having this conversation with you." Russell held his hands up in surrender, "But, I can't ignore pack law."

"Meaning?" Rose asked warily.

"Meaning," Russell sighed and gave her a look of sympathy. "Meaning, that a lone wolf seduced a pack female."

"It was a mutual seduction, I made my choice," Rose argued.

Russell held up his hands again to silence her.

"I'm going to pretend I didn't hear that, Rose. Pack law states that he be punished for his actions, however, considering what you have told me about him saving your life, as the soon-to-be new Alpha, I am willing to let him go without pursuing him. If you had played an active part in the seduction, then, Rose, I would have to banish you. I don't want to do that." He held out his hand in invitation for her to take it in hers. She refused it, so he rubbed his sweating palms down over his jeans instead.

"Your place in the Darkhills pack was under enough jeopardy before all this nasty business,"

Russell explained. "The fact remains that if you are not mated soon, you won't be welcome here anymore."

"So, I'm facing banishment one way or another," Rose said bitterly.

"Rose, you've got to understand, I *have* to uphold our laws, especially this one. It was made by the pack Alpha way back when you were just a cub. Sam might not have been a good leader, but his father is still upheld as one of the greatest wolves in Darkhills' history. I can't go against his law."

"So, my options are, to find a mate within Darkhills or leave, is that what you're saying?"

"It's not quite so easy as that now, Rose." Russell sighed heavily. "I'm sorry, sweetheart, but now that you've been with a lone wolf, you'll be unlikely to find a male within the pack who will want you." He cringed as he said it.

"Are you kidding me? So, what, I'm damaged goods now, is that it?" Rose's anger was like a hot wave that threatened to flood the room.

"It's shit, Rose. I know, trust me I wish things were different." He ran his hands through his hair in frustration. "So many of our laws and customs are outdated but the pack still values the old ways and traditions. I can't start trying to change that until I've established myself as Alpha, even then it's going to take a long time."

"So, what? Are you telling me to leave?" Rose asked, the thought of leaving her grandmother and friends was like a looming dark pit of despair.

She had lost her mate and now it looked like she was going to lose everything else she held dear. Despite her best efforts to keep her feelings in check, rogue tears started to spill down her face. She refused to let out the sob that was prying at her throat.

Russell cursed and snatched her up into his arms. His embrace was hard and cold, offering zero comfort and Rose stiffened against him. Despite that, he continued to hush and coo in her ear.

"Oh hell, sweetheart. I can't stand to see you cry. I've always liked you, Rose, ever since I joined the pack. I'd never want to see you hurt."

"It's fine Russ, I understand. You have a job to do. Just give me a little time to set up someplace to go and I'll be gone." She choked out from where he still held her against his chest.

"Wait, Rose, listen." Russell suddenly held her at arm's length and looked deeply into her eyes. "I know you've never thought of me in that way, but I promise I'd treat you well. You'd want for nothing."

"What? What are you saying?" Rose stammered.

Her head spun in confusion.

"Mate *me*, Rose, and I swear I'll do my best to give you happiness. You could stay in the pack, hell you'd lead Darkhills by my side as Luna. I'd make sure your grandmother got the best care as she grew older and maybe one day," He paused and took a deep breath, a small smile tilting at the corners of his lips. "Maybe one day you can find happiness in raising our cubs."

"What?" Rose repeated dumbly. "Why? Why would you do that? You said males wouldn't be interested in me, why would you want me? You're going to be Alpha."

"I like you, Rose." He blushed deeply and gave her a shy smile. "I've always liked you and I want to take this pack into a new era, what better way for me to do that than leading by example, with an unconventional choice for a mate by my side?"

Rose felt the sting of his words. 'An unconventional mate'. That is exactly how she'd be viewed by the pack. She'd be talked about. She probably already *was* being talked about with people judging her for having slept with a lone wolf. Annoyance and anger coursed through her. They all thought lone wolves were such bad creatures, but they had no idea about the reality. The worst monsters lurked within their precious traditional communities.

But Russ said he wanted to make things better.

Rose cared about her pack, about the people in it. They were her family, she owed them everything and she wanted to help them thrive. If she stayed, she could expose Sam's thievery and help to rebuild a better way of life for the pack. She could stay with her friends and support them as they grew their families. She'd be able to stay close to her grandma and take care of her. The only thing that waited for her in a life outside of the pack was loneliness and somewhere out there, her True Mate. A True Mate that had made it clear that he didn't want her.

She would love Cayden Greystone, until her dying breath even if he had never loved her back. But she could fill her life with love for the others around her. Maybe one day she would grow to care for Russell, if he showed himself to be the fair and considerate Alpha that he so promised.

With a silent nod, she answered him.

"Was that a yes, Rose?" Russell asked. He clutched her hands tightly, excitement and victory lighting up his brown eyes.

"Yes, Russell," She said quietly, unable to look him in the eye, choosing to stare down at their joined hands. "I'll be your mate."

Deep within her, tucked up small, her wolf let

out a tiny whimper, the fight having completely left her. She blinked slowly and continued to stare into the darkness.

# CHAPTER NINETEEN

## *Cayden*

Cayden woke from his fitful dreams, with the feeling of being watched.

He shook away the vision of Rose in trouble from his dreams and peered into the darkness of the room, growling in a warning.

"Now, now, there is no need for that," Lucian Nightingale tutted from where he sat in one of the leather chesterfields.

"You'll have to forgive me; I don't take too kindly to being watched while I sleep," Cayden replied, his voice still a deep gravel.

"Quite," Lucian agreed. "However, I couldn't listen to your whimpering and whining for a moment longer." He stood and glided to the light switch, flicking it on.

The sudden illumination made Cayden curse as he squinted against the light.

"Whining?"

"Yes. You were making quite a disturbance upon my evening; anyone would think you were in distress." He leaned casually against the door frame with his arms crossed over his chest, casting his dark eyes over Cayden. "However, upon investigation, you appear to be in a decent enough state, I suppose."

Cayden huffed at the man. Lucian Nightingale was a snob. While Cayden might not dress in the expensive designer suits that the man preferred, he never considered himself to be unkempt. Although if he were truthful, he was wearing stale old clothes that he usually kept crumpled up in his gym bag and still hadn't gotten around to shaving his beard.

Lucian on the other hand stood nonchalantly against the wall in a tailored black suit, crisp white, open-collared shirt and shoes that shone. He was clean-shaven, likely to show off his jawline that could cut like a knife, and had his thick black hair cropped short at the sides and longer on top. A raised, superior brow let Cayden know he knew exactly what he was thinking.

He should probably clean up before they got down to talking business. Cayden rose from the bed and walked towards the tub in the corner of the room.

"I wouldn't bother. I believe your current appearance will work nicely for the task I have in mind."

"Whatever it is, I'm in," Cayden said gruffly.

He needed to keep himself distracted from thinking about Rose. He was finding it hard to shake a feeling of foreboding regarding his mate. *Not my mate.* He needed to stop thinking of her like that. He had let her go. He had no claim over her now.

"That is unlike you." Lucian frowned.

"Why does it matter?" Cayden countered.

"You've always wanted to know intimate details of any contracts I propose. Your thoroughness and sense of morality has always been one of your most admirable qualities," Lucian replied honestly.

"Well, I no longer care. What's the job?" Cayden asked. He didn't want to waste any more time.

"I need you to kill a man," Lucian stated, inspecting his fingernails.

"Done." Cayden pushed his feelings down. "Won't be my first kill this week."

He was a bad wolf; it was about time he just embraced it.

"See now, this is what I mean," Lucian said in frustration, pushing off from the wall. "The wolf I invited here wouldn't have accepted such a job." He opened the door to the room and strode out. "I want to know what has changed."

Cayden clenched his fists at his side.

"Since when did you care about morality," He replied, as he stepped out onto the balcony.

"You'll have to come down here, Mr. Greystone. I'm afraid I can't make sense of your growling from this distance."

Cayden's mouth dropped. Lucian was sat in his usual spot at the end of the great hall, the floor below.

*How the hell?*

"Come, Come. I haven't got all night."

Cayden refused to scurry down the stairs to meet with the condescending asshole, so he took a step back and launched himself over the side of the balustrade, landing soundly in a crouched position in front of him. He slowly straightened and lifted his head to meet Lucian's gaze. The guy didn't even raise a brow at his entrance.

"Now, why do you suddenly have no qualms about taking a man's life, without a reason?"

"Things change."

"Indeed. As can my opinion of a person." Lucian absently rearranged the cuffs beneath his suit sleeves. "Allow me to elucidate, Mr. Greystone, I do not look to hire people haphazardly. I like to be able to trust those with whom I associate. You are acting out of character which threatens the trust that I have in you." Lucian steepled his hands in front of him and sat back in his chair. "So, I'll ask you once more: What has changed? Perhaps the answer lies with this other murder you mentioned?"

"It wasn't murder. It was a justified killing," Cayden corrected, despite himself.

"I see. Justified in what way?"

"I killed a wolf for attempting to force a female to mate," Cayden replied.

"Ah, I understand, very heroic. This would be the female I can smell upon your person, yes?"

Cayden remained quiet, refusing to give in to the urge to draw in the scent of his mate that still clung to him.

"You're not the only creature with a keen sense of smell. Mine may not be as good as a wolf's but it serves me well enough." Lucian kept his bored gaze on his steepled fingers. "The female, is she yours? Have I missed an invitation to a mating ceremony?"

Lucian tutted.

"She is with her pack, where she belongs. I am a lone wolf, Lucian, as you well know. I do not mate."

"Well, that is a ridiculous notion. I have known many a lone wolf to be mated in my time." Lucian scoffed and looked at Cayden with inky eyes that seemed to bore into him, searching for answers. The feeling was unpleasant yet, Cayden refused to look away.

"What does this have to do with the job?" Cayden ground out, trying to rein in his frustration all the while wondering why his chest felt so tight.

"Your soul is heavier than the last time we met, Cayden. You've borne the tragedies of your past on your shoulders since I've known you, but this goes deeper. This burden weighs more." Lucian held Cayden's gaze, and his pride be damned he wanted to break the contact. Only he physically couldn't. His wolf whined and bent his head low while all Cayden could do was gasp as it felt as though his entire being was being held in a tight grasp.

"I don't deserve her," He wheezed out, the words coming out of their own volition. All of a sudden, the sensation stopped, and Lucian looked away as if bored.

"Nonsense. Why ever not?"

"What the?" Cayden choked out. "What the hell did you just do to me?"

"Answer my question and perhaps I'll answer yours." Lucian smiled wickedly as he took out his phone and looked at the screen briefly before returning it to his inside pocket.

"For fuck sake Lucian!" Cayden growled out. "Because all I ever do is hurt people. My mother died because of me. My father was driven insane because of me. My pack is better off without me and Rose will be better off without me."

"Forgive me for picking apart your argument, however," Lucian turned to face him. "You did not kill your mother. Rockslides happen. It was an unfortunate tragedy. Your father was weak-willed for not being able to honour the memory of his mate by caring for you, instead, he wrongly blamed you. From what I know, you were nothing but loyal and beloved by your pack. And finally, while I may not be an expert in wolf customs, I know that love is rare and worth fighting for."

"How do you know about my pack, about me?" Cayden asked, shock ricocheting through him.

He expected Lucian to be the kind of man who ran checks on his employees, but this level of information was intrusive and personal.

"Who do you think your father asked to save your mother all those years ago?"

Cayden couldn't believe it. Lucian was as young as he was, both males in their prime. How could he be the ancient one his father had pleaded with? But as he looked at Lucian, he could find no hint of trickery. His dark eyes shone with matter-of-fact honesty.

A hundred questions flew through his mind as he continued to watch the man in front of him. None of which would help him in his current situation. Cayden had tried hard to leave the past where it was. And right now, he needed to convince Lucian that he was still the right man for the job. He needed the distraction, facing a future with nothing but the emptiness left by his mate to occupy his mind was not an option. He'd go insane.

"Love is not so simple," Cayden said into the silence. "It's because I love her that I walked away, it was the only thing I could do."

"Must I repeat myself? We've already established that you aren't the Big Bad Wolf you think yourself to be," Lucian waved a bored hand in front of his face.

"They were going to kill her. If I had stayed, if I had returned to the Darkhills pack with her, the Beta said he'd kill us both."

"The Darkhills pack?" Lucian sat up at that. "This wolf you killed, it didn't happen to be the Alpha, did it?"

"Yes, why?"

"Oh, that explains the sudden invitation I have to attend the Alpha ascension tonight." Lucian raised his hand and clicked once, the serious-looking butler from before appeared from the shadows, "Bring me the invitation from the Darkhills pack."

The man disappeared on silent feet.

"I wasn't aware you were so cosy with the pack," Cayden said, a small part of him fearful that Lucian's loyalties were with the pack, therefore not with him.

"I'm not. Their previous Alpha, the one you killed, was keen to engage me in business, but I've never had much interest in anything that forest town had to offer. It would appear the prospective new Alpha wishes to continue to court me."

The butler returned and passed Lucian a card upon a small silver tray. He plucked it up with a leisurely swipe of his fingers and held it in front of him for a moment before returning it to the tray and dismissing the servant.

"My mistake, it is an Alpha ascension and

mating ceremony combined. The Darkhills pack is getting both a new Alpha and Luna tonight, some she-wolf named Rose."

Cayden roared out his fury, unable to hold back the fierce rage that slammed into him.

"That son-of-a-bitch!"

"My, my! Mr. Greystone, such a temper. Am I to assume your lovely lady wolf's name is Rose Woods?"

"I'll kill him," Cayden snarled.

"Yes, yes, you do seem to have a penchant for killing the Alphas of the Darkhills pack." Lucian leaned back in his chair and crossed his leg over the other while Cayden paced. "Tell me, why is it you'll be killing this one?"

"Because she's mine."

"I see. How very possessive of you. I'm not entirely sure the female would appreciate being considered property. Let's see if you can't improve on that statement, perhaps thinking as Cayden rather than as your wolf." Lucian rebuked, resting his chin on his closed fist.

"Because I love her."

"That is more like it. Off you go then, go kill another Alpha and kiss and make up with your female." He dismissed.

"I can't," Cayden growled out his frustration and fought to keep his wolf in check.

"Why not?"

"He said they'd kill her if I returned. I can't fight off a whole pack."

"I have every confidence in your abilities, Mr. Greystone, however, why exactly would you need to fight the entire Darkhills pack? Surely you just need to fight the Beta?" Lucian asked, cocking his head to one side.

The solution was obvious and hit Cayden like a freight train.

"Alpha challenge."

"Indeed. Who better to do it than a Greystone who is fighting for his mate?" Lucian asked.

"Lucian, I have to go," Cayden called over his shoulder as he started half-jogging down the hall. "I'm sorry about your job, but you'll have to find someone else to kill your man."

"Oh, that," Lucian said, appearing beside Cayden in a blur of movement too fast for him to see. Cayden jumped to the side slightly at his apparition. "That was never the job. I just wanted to find out what had made you go dead inside. I'll hire another for the task I had in mind."

"Okay... Thanks." Cayden muttered, too desperate to get back to Darkhills territory to be mad.

"Don't thank me just yet," Lucian continued. "I had your vehicle towed."

"You what?!" Cayden growled at the man grabbing him by the collar of his suit jacket.

"I told you I didn't like it." Lucian shrugged himself out of Cayden's grip with ease. "Don't fret. We'll be taking mine." He lifted his keys out of his pocket and jingled them in the air as he continued towards the doors.

He swept his other hand to the side and the heavy wooden doors swung open as if by his command. Cayden's mouth dropped open, as realization dawned on him as to who or what his elusive business associate truly was.

Lucian glanced back over his shoulder and flashed him a fanged grin.

"Come, come, we wouldn't want to be too late to save your beloved Rose," said the vampire.

# CHAPTER TWENTY

## *Rose*

Rose stared absently out of the window of her friend's truck, into the dark night sky. Clint and Carly had agreed to drive her to the ceremonial clearing in the forest.

Traditionally she'd be arriving with her parents. But it had long been the case that was a tradition she would never enjoy. With her grandfather gone and her grandma in the hospital, she couldn't even be presented by them. Her friends were driving her there, but she would present herself for mating.

She searched within herself again. Her wolf didn't even lift her head.

No. None of this was what Rose wanted, but even worse was the prospect of having to leave her family, her friends and the only home she'd ever known. Rose had resigned herself to never having what she wanted again. She'd never have her True Mate. She'd had a taste of him, and it had been the most exquisite joy she had ever known. That would have to be enough to last her for a lifetime of sacrificing her happiness for the sake of those she loved.

She'd agreed with Russell to have a joint mating ceremony and ascension ceremony that night, it was either that or wait for another lunar cycle for the next full moon. Rose just wanted it done.

"My mating ceremony dress looks good on you Rose," Carly offered quietly from where she sat beside her in the back seat of Clint's truck.

Rose looked down at the pale pink gown and considered it once more. It had looked beautiful on her friend, its floating tulle skirt and sparkling bodice suited Carly's soft and loving personality. She remembered how it had seemed to reflect the happy glow of her friend's smile as she had stood and said her vows with Clint. Rose wasn't sure she would do the dress justice tonight.

"I mean, you'll need to hitch it up a bit when you walk seeing as you wouldn't let me shorten it, but you look pretty," Carly continued.

"There was no way I was going to let you attack your mating gown with scissors for this thing," Rose admonished.

"This *thing*?" Carly half sobbed. "Oh Rose, this isn't right. You don't love him. Mating should be for love. Why don't you call it off? We could say you weren't feeling well, that you're still recovering from everything that happened."

Rose shook her head.

"She's right, Rose," Clint chipped in from the front seat, his eyes meeting hers in the rear-view mirror. "This doesn't feel right. Tell me to turn this car around now and I'll do it."

"Thank you both, but I'm doing it," Rose said firmly. "Not all mating matches are made for love. Some are out of obligation. Some are out of necessity. I need to cement my loyalty to Darkhills, and I need to be a part of making this pack a better place. Russ told me he wanted to make changes. I can't be a part of that if I'm not a Darkhills wolf." She sucked in a fortifying breath. "So tonight, I am mating Russ."

Clint cursed under his breath and Carly didn't even try to hide her tears.

Rose turned her head, to once again stare out of the window as she tried to ignore the occasional hushed proclamations that the situation wasn't fair from the seat beside her.

*Life isn't fair*. Rose thought bitterly.

If life was fair, her parents would've raised her to adulthood instead of dying so young. If life was fair her grandfather would never have gotten cancer. If life was fair, she would've met Cayden Greystone at some kind of pack diplomacy meeting, and they could've fallen in love and courted the traditional way. They could've been mated in a shining ceremony with everyone she ever loved there to witness her happiness at finding her True Mate. If life was fair, they would've had a future together, full of family, friendship, laughter and love.

Her fantasy was abruptly brought to and end by the sight of the other pack members' trucks lined up in the makeshift parking lot. A row of sparsely placed flaming torches lit the way towards the ceremonial circle. Clint pulled on the brake and killed the engine.

"Last chance, Rose," he said, turning in his seat to look at her. "If you want out, I'll drive us straight back out of here, just say the word." His steady and caring face was something of a comfort to her.

"Russ may not be the wolf I love, but he's a nice guy. There are worse fates than being his mate," she said, trying hard to keep the tremble from her voice. She had promised herself that she wouldn't cry.

"It's Cayden, isn't it? You love him don't you, hon? *He's* your True Mate," Carly asked, gingerly reaching for Rose's cold hand.

She sucked in a breath at hearing his name and looked to the roof of the truck, blinking away the tears.

"Please don't talk about him," she pleaded, turning her head to look at her friend. The sadness she saw there reflected her own.

"Oh, Rose." Carly shook her head and squeezed her hand tightly. "I'm so sorry."

Refusing to give in to the misery that threatened to overwhelm her, Rose sniffed loudly and cleared her throat. She needed to get through tonight, and then she could work on making the best of her situation.

"It's fine. Let's go." She pulled her hand from Carly's and let herself out of the truck, hoisting the soft skirt of the dress up as she climbed down.

She was sure as hell glad she had refused the offer of high heels; her dusty, brown kicks were far better for her resolute stomp towards the ceremonial circle. The hurried footsteps of her friends behind her gave her a small boost of courage.

"At least the ascension ceremony is happening before Russel and I tie the knot," She said, with false cheerfulness. "Most of the pack will be too occupied with wanting to congratulate Russ on becoming

Alpha than worrying about whether I'm enjoying my wedding day."

Carly sniffed sadly behind her.

"That's enough now, Carls. She's made up her mind. She needs our strength, not our tears," Clint hushed quietly, almost too low for Rose to hear. "You can cry on me as much as you like later."

Rose smiled softly to herself. They might fight and fuss sometimes, but Clint and Carly complemented each other in the sweetest of ways. Their love for one another was obvious for all to see.

They reached the entrance to the ceremonial circle and Rose cast a nervous glance around the tree line that ringed the empty space. The entire pack was there. Every set of eyes looked towards the centre of the clearing where Russell stood waiting. He was clearly not prepared to start the ceremony until everyone had arrived. Including his future mate. His eyes met hers before looking towards some chairs that had been set out to one side of the clearing, he glanced back at her and nodded once in encouragement.

She had hoped to just blend in with the rest of the pack. She didn't want to be the centre of attention for any longer than completely necessary. However, Russell clearly expected her to take a seat for all to see and watch him ascend.

Even as she stepped out into the clearing, her entire being rebelled. She didn't want any of this. But as a ripple of voices grew around her, she knew she had no choice but to keep putting one foot in front of the other.

To her surprise, most of the voices were soft coos of awe or sighs of joy. Rose carefully took her seat and scanned the crowd once more. People were smiling. She wasn't hated like she expected or like Russell had implied that she would be. A frown creased her brow a moment before the voice of the eldest wolf of the pack rang out to the crowd.

"Darkhills, tonight sees the dawning of a new era for our pack."

The crowd hushed their murmurings and listened intently.

"Russell Drayton joined our pack nearly ten years ago. He has since been our Beta, a loyal and stalwart second to his cousin, Sam McClaw. With the sad passing of his blood kin, he now seeks to ascend to the position of Alpha."

*Cousin?!* Both Rose and her wolf sat up at that. How had she not known the two of them were related? A sense of dread filled her.

"The laws of our pack and every wolf pack

throughout history dictate that we consider all and any challenges to this ascension. So, if there are any among you who wish to challenge our long-established Beta, you have until the rising of the full moon at its highest to stake your claim."

Silence echoed in the clearing, cold and crisp.

Rose cursed inwardly. *Please, someone challenge. Please.*

"Our Beta will now address us with his declaration."

The elder wolf shuffled back to the tree line and merged with the rest of the crowd.

"Darkhills," Russell's voice broke the silence once more. "While I mourn the loss of my Alpha, my cousin and my friend Sam McClaw, I have been given a gift by the moon goddess in the opportunity to honour his good name and the way in which he led our pack, by taking on the mantle of leadership."

*Honour his good name? What the hell?* Rose listened in shock as Russell continued to lay praise upon Sam, despite everything that she had told him.

"His death was untimely but befitting of the kind of Alpha he was. He died trying to protect one of our own. I am only thankful that no serious harm was done to my dearly betrothed." Russell swept his arm towards Rose and made a dramatic show of clutching at his heart. "The thought of almost losing her as well as Sam is just too much to think about."

Rose's wolf was growling low and slowly getting to her feet as fury built within her.

"I have ensured that the abomination that sought to take her from me, that struck an elder of this pack and murdered our Alpha, dare not ever return. For if he does, I will see the lone wolf skinned alive for what he tried to do to the Darkhills pack."

The crowd continued to talk in hushed whispers, making what they would of Russell's speech.

"As your Alpha, I will continue the good work of Sam McClaw and will protect the Darkhills from those outsiders who would seek to destroy us."

"Sam McClaw was a rapist and crook!" Rose shouted out, to the crowd.

The murmurs intensified around her and Russell shot her an angry glare. She refused to be intimidated. The Darkhills pack deserved to hear the truth about their Alpha and the truth about Cayden.

"Our Alpha didn't die protecting me," she

continued, striding into the centre of the clearing to address her pack. "He died because he tried to rape me. He tried to force me to mate with him. The lone wolf, whose name is Cayden by the way, saved my life."

"Please, everyone, please excuse this outburst." Russell held up his hands to hush the frenzied voices of the pack. "My betrothed has experienced significant trauma, the doctors with whom I have consulted, believe she has confused the events in her mind as a coping mechanism to help her survive her time as the lone wolf's captive."

"What the hell? That's bullshit," Rose cursed at him.

"It's OK Rose," he soothed with a gentle tone that didn't reach his eyes. "You're safe now. You're here with me, Russell." He tried to pull her into his embrace, but she refused to go, shoving him away angrily, and spitting at him.

"Don't you touch me," she hissed.

Russell wiped at his face and made a dramatic sigh to the crowd.

"As you can see, she's quite delusional and distressed. The sooner we are mated, the sooner I can arrange for the best doctors and the best medicines to help her get better."

"I am not delusional. Ask my grandmother. She saw the whole thing; she'll tell you what Sam McClaw did to her and what he tried to do to me."

"That won't be possible, Rose, the lone wolf hurt her so badly that she is in a coma. Don't you remember?" Russell countered, his syrupy sweet voice oozing over her.

"No, she isn't!" Came a voice from the crowd. Carly pushed her way forward to the front and glared at Russell. "Clint and I spoke to her in the hospital today, and I bet she'd have a thing or two to say to you right now, Russell Drayton."

"This is ridiculous," Russell shouted above the raucous crowd. "From this moment on I declare that females are not permitted to speak during ascension ceremonies."

"You're not Alpha yet," Clint spoke up from beside Carly, the two of them standing with their chins lifted in defiance.

"I've not heard anyone offer a challenge?" Russell laughed. "And I know you haven't got the nerve, not unless you want to lose that shitty little house that you call home."

Rose looked on in horror as the flicker of fear and shame entered her friend's eyes, and he stayed silent. Biting at his lip to keep from replying.

"You've been blackmailing him," Rose bit out.

"Sweetheart, I've been blackmailing the entire Darkhills pack. Nice of you to finally catch on."

"You won't get away with this," Rose growled.

Russell shrugged and returned his attention to goading her friends.

"I'd suggest you downsize to a trailer," Russell mocked. "Only I hear those things tend to be rather flammable. Not exactly suitable for a family home. Oh, no wait, it's still just the two of you. How long is it you've been mated now?" He sneered at Clint. "That's why you won't challenge me, you clearly don't have the balls for it."

"You son-of-a-bitch." Carly tried to launch herself into the clearing, while Clint grappled with her to hold her back.

Russell continued to laugh.

"At least someone's got some fight in that pairing. It's a shame females aren't permitted to challenge for Alpha, I wouldn't mind throwing it down with her."

Clint's fangs erupted at that and a dark snarl escaped his lips.

Russell turned his back, unperturbed and

chuckled as he looked up into the sky at the full moon that shone overhead.

"Well, looks like it is almost time for me to ascend, and I think this Alpha's in the mood for a little banishment."

The roar of an engine filled the clearing as a sleek black sports car skidded to a halt at the entrance to the ceremonial circle. Rose's heart leapt as in the next moment, her mate climbed out and strode into the centre of the clearing, going toe to toe with Russell.

"I challenge for Alpha."

# CHAPTER TWENTY-ONE

*Cayden*

"We have a challenge," the elder called out to the assembled Darkhills pack. "State your name, wolf, and your reason for challenging for Alpha status."

"I am Cayden Greystone, formally of the Greystone pack," Cayden called out, not once taking his eyes from the pathetic wolf standing in front of him. The murmur from the crowd at the mention of his name didn't go unnoticed by him. "I challenge for Alpha to give the female Rose Woods and the Darkhills pack its freedom from this poor excuse of a wolf."

The murmuring crowd grew louder, and he heard a few voices make cautious remarks in his favour. They were fearful still of the Beta. He would show them he wasn't worth fearing.

"This is... ridiculous," Russell stammered as he walked backwards. "It's too late. The moon is high."

"I understood that a wolf could challenge for Alpha status at any time," Lucian corrected in his usual condescending tone as he walked up behind Cayden.

"The challenge is valid," The elder confirmed.

"This wolf is not welcome in the Darkhills," Russell spoke to the crowd. "And who even is *this* guy? Humans are not permitted at ceremonies."

"I'd remember your manners if I were you, and I believe you invited him," Cayden replied curtly. "Lord Lucian Nightingale, meet the Darkhills Beta."

"Charmed I'm sure." Lucian waved a dismissive hand and glided towards Rose who stood as a soft pink blur in his peripherals. He didn't trust himself to look at her yet, and he didn't trust Russell not to try anything underhand, so he kept his focus. But he could scent her relief and he could hear her wolf calling out to him in greeting.

*Yes, my love, I'm here.*

"My dear, I believe it would be better if you were to retreat to a safer distance." Lucian held out his arm for Rose to take.

"I'd rather stay here and watch him go down," she gritted out, turning her furious eyes back to Russell.

Oh, that was so much like his mate, not scared of a little fight, keen to see justice done.

Lucian chuckled.

"You'll have a better view from over here." He gently guided her towards the tree line where Cayden heard her friends rushing to greet her.

"Russell Drayton, do you accept the challenge?" The elder called out to the hushed crowd.

"Of course I don't accept it; it's ludicrous. Since when were criminals permitted to challenge?" Russell blustered.

"So, you yield?" The elder questioned.

"No, I do not yield. This pack belongs to me, I have spent the last ten years waiting for my turn, no one is going to take it from me," Russell barked out.

"The challenge is accepted then," the elder called out. "Darkhills, the laws of a challenge dictate that each wolf must have a second. Should a contender be unable to continue, their second is permitted to fight in their stead. Wolves, please ask your seconds to come forward now."

A tremor of doubt coursed through Cayden. Who did he have here that would vouch for him enough to fight by his side? Russell fixed him with a knowing look as if he were about to enjoy seeing him humiliated.

"I call Taymour Moss as my second," Russell called out smugly, his Beta influence filtered through the air at his announcement.

While using influence during a challenge was permitted, it was expected that it would be used during the fight, often to finally subdue an opponent.

A huge beast of a man reluctantly strode forward to stand behind Russell. He was broad and his biceps strained beneath his shirt. The man clearly didn't feel comfortable with being called forward but had been summoned by his Beta's influence, so had submitted.

Cayden wouldn't force a wolf to fight for him. He was confident he could easily take down the other wolf without a second but if needed, he would ask Lucian to step in. He wasn't sure if asking another creature to act as second was permitted. He didn't think it had ever happened before.

With every passing second, his hopes of having a wolf from the Darkhills pack volunteer as his second began to dwindle.

"I second this wolf," Rose's voice called out into the clearing.

"Rose, No," The words left Cayden's mouth on instinct.

"Females are not permitted to enter an Alpha challenge," Russell sneered.

"I'm afraid he is right my dear, though your bravery is admirable. Your grandparents would be proud," The elder confirmed, his eyes softening as he spoke to her.

"Never mind, my dear." Lucian gently placed his hands on her shoulders and guided her back a step. "Besides, your mate would most likely have my head if I were to let anything happen to you."

*He's not wrong*, thought Cayden.

"I will second this wolf."

Cayden turned in surprise to see Clint striding forward.

"And I'll fight for the same reasons; for Rose's freedom and for the freedom of the pack. Cayden Greystone is exactly the kind of wolf that Darkhills needs." He stood by Cayden's side and nodded his allegiance, "And also because Russell is an asshole." He added with a wink.

Cayden smirked. The warmth that radiated from his chest was unexpected. He had come to the challenge to save Rose and then planned to abdicate like he had before. He never expected to find loyalty and acceptance. He had always thought he would never be worthy of such things.

"Let me know if you need a third!" The voice of Nate rang out from the crowd, followed by rumbles of agreement from numerous other wolves.

Russell growled his annoyance.

"There is no such thing as 'Thirds', Nathaniel, though I'm sure your willingness is appreciated." The elder replied sternly.

"Seconds, take your place at the edge of the circle," the elder continued. "Contenders, prepare yourselves."

Russell skulked off towards the tree line and began hopping and shuffling out of his clothes, fussing with them before hurriedly shifting into a lean and hungry-looking russet-coloured wolf.

Cayden kept his eyes on his opponent as he kicked off his boots and, pulled his shirt off over his head. He eyed the other wolf as it trotted its way into the clearing, assessing it for its potential strengths and weaknesses.

He shifted, leaving his clothes in a pile at the edge of the clearing. And tried to ignore the murmurs of approval as his huge ebony black animal paced slowly into the centre. His wolf was a formidable sight.

The elder stood at the centre of the ring and held up his wrinkled hands for silence.

"Wolves, you are here to fight for the status of Alpha of the Darkhills pack. Fights to the death are permitted, but to be avoided. A beaten wolf should yield when they are unable to fight any longer. The challenge will continue until a winner is declared."

Russell's wolf's eyes shifted nervously around as he faced off with Cayden. He understood why. He was an average-sized wolf with little muscle. Cayden was almost twice his size and kept his body honed. Despite potentially having the home crowd behind him, the odds were not stacked in the Beta's favour and he knew it.

"Let the challenge commence," the elder announced.

Before the man had a chance to step away, Russell launched himself at the elder, using his head to knock the man down in front of Cayden's wolf, before retreating to the far edges of the ring to stalk around him.

The horrified gasp of the crowd echoed throughout the clearing. Cayden cursed as he bent his head low and sniffed at the old man. He wasn't badly injured, more shocked by the fiendish wolf's actions. No others were permitted to enter the circle while the challenge took place. Cayden needed to see the elderly man to safety before he could take care of his opponent.

With gentle nudges, he lifted the old man, encouraging him to lean his weight over Cayden's body, and with steady steps, he carried him over to the crowd. The pack applauded and cheered him as he came closer, the elder breathing heavily in his ear as he lumbered on.

"Thank you, son," the elder wheezed as he was gathered up into the arms of his pack.

Cayden didn't have a chance to respond as Russell's wolf launched at his hind legs, biting down. A snarl ripped from Cayden's throat and he spun around and snapped at the russet-coloured wolf. He released his hold immediately and tried to retreat, but Cayden was too fast and within a few long strides, he pounced on his back.

The wolf whined as Cayden's claws dug into his flesh. He fell to the ground and rolled, taking Cayden's wolf with him. The two wrestled and clawed at each other in the dirt for a moment before Cayden's wolf claimed the upper hand and with his heavy paw pressed against Russell's throat, he growled down at him, his teeth bared in a warning.

They stayed like that for a minute, before Russell's wolf looked away in submission.

A cheer went up from the crowd and Cayden released Russell. The victorious shouts turned into ones of outrage as Russell suddenly kicked up the dirt into Cayden's eyes, temporarily blinding him. Then it was Cayden's turn to go down as Russell launched himself at him.

A blinding pain in his shoulder let him know that Russell had got a good bite in. With a snarl Cayden pushed himself to his feet and slammed his body down, landing on top of Russell. With a yelp of pain, the wolf released Cayden's shoulder.

Wasting no time, Cayden sunk his teeth into his opponent's neck and with a heave of his head, swung the wolf across the clearing. Its body landed with a thud and the snap of bones breaking could be heard through his howl of agony.

As Cayden's wolf paced over to the prostrated animal, he watched it shift back into the human form of Russell.

"I call upon my second to fight in my stead," he called out in panic.

The crowd growled out its displeasure as the huge man from before entered the circle and carried a moaning Russell to the edge of the ring. Cayden wasn't surprised the Beta had tapped out. If anything, he had expected him to do so earlier. His black wolf watched as the other wolf sent him an apologetic shrug before shucking off his clothes and shifting into a vast brown timber wolf.

This wolf was bigger than his own, so it was time to change tactics. Using his immense speed Cayden's wolf charged at his new opponent and sent it tumbling. Just as he suspected, while this wolf was powerful, he lacked speed.

The large shaggy wolf shook his head and gathered itself to its feet to face off with Cayden. The two circled each other, looking for their next opening. Cayden noticed that the wolf was giving him ample opportunities. The wolf had no intention of winning the fight.

The next turn, when the larger wolf showed his back to Cayden, he sprung. The wolf went down easily and submitted.

Just when he thought it was finally over, Rose's cry of horror cut through the cheers of the crowd and Cayden felt a sharp blade plunge into his side. He reared back and swiped with his paws, knocking Russell in his human form to the ground.

The knife jutted out from his side, his blood slowly seeping out as he watched Russell try to scurry to his feet only to be held down by his second. The Beta had overtly broken the rules of the challenge by attacking in human form and with a weapon. The challenge was over. Cayden had won.

*Stay down.*

Cayden sent the command to Russell and watched as he submitted to his influence.

Soft hands tugged at Cayden's fur and he looked up to see Rose, desperately trying to inspect his knife wound through his thick pelt. Tears rolled down her face as she looked at him.

"Cayden, no." She choked on a sob and threw herself at his head, pulling his face to hers.

He had so much to say to his mate, but first, he needed to address his new pack.

He nuzzled her gently and gave a soft lick to her tear-stained cheeks before he backed away from her. With a gut-wrenching howl of pain, Cayden shifted into his human form, the blade still deep within his side, and with a mighty effort, he heaved himself to his feet and stood.

"Darkhills, I, Cayden Greystone, claim the title of Alpha, I vow to protect and uphold our laws and with every action I take as your Alpha, I will strengthen and rebuild this pack to its rightful glory. You will have my loyalty, my dedication and my honour." His deep voice echoed out among the clearing. Every set of eyes were on him.

"My first action as your Alpha is to abolish the outdated law that demands that the female Rose

Woods mate to secure her place within Darkhills. From this moment, she is a full member, and her choice of mate is entirely hers."

A loud cheer went up around him and he finally turned to take in the beauty of his mate. Her auburn hair was coming loose from its pins and her mascara had run with her tears, but her eyes shone with joy.

"What if I want to mate with a Darkhills wolf?" She asked, jutting her chin out in defiance, her hands resting on her hips.

Sadness struck his heart with an agony that went beyond what he had endured during the challenge. With a heavy sigh, he replied.

"You may choose whomever you wish, I want only for you to be happy, Rose, but please know that I'll always consider you to be my one True Mate."

"Good," she said curtly before throwing herself into his arms.

A chorus of jubilant howls and cheers went up all around them as Cayden caught her with a surprised grunt of pain as the blade twisted slightly in his side. At that moment he couldn't care less. Her lips had crashed onto his and his mate was kissing him with a passion that knew no bounds.

He growled low in his throat and tangled his

fingers in her hair, pulling her tighter against him so he could plunder her mouth with his desperate tongue.

*How did I ever think I could be without her?*

A throat cleared awkwardly beside him, letting Cayden know Lucian had appeared. A wicked thought flitted through his mind and he decided to prolong the snob's discomfort by taking his time to kiss his mate for a while longer, coaxing her tongue to join his in a languid and sinful dance.

"Oh, for heaven's sake," Lucian cursed, and Cayden finally released his mate's mouth and turned to grin at his friend.

"Honestly, I will never understand how wolves are so comfortable with exposing their naked bodies. Especially considering your current state of arousal." Lucian tutted as he circled around Cayden and prodded at his injured shoulder, then bent to inspect the knife buried in his side.

"My dear Miss Woods, would you mind terribly if I were to ask you to take a step back from Mr. Greystone? Perhaps he would appreciate his clothes? And I wouldn't want you to risk getting any more mess on your friend's dress."

"What makes you think it's not mine?" Rose asked as she, stepped away slightly affronted.

"A lady of your colouring would look better in greens and blues; it would highlight those mesmerizing eyes." Lucian shot her a dashing smile making her instantly blush at the compliment. Cayden growled. "That and it's approximately six inches too long for you."

Rose laughed at that.

"You're not wrong." She turned and gave Cayden one more soft kiss. "I'll be back with your clothes; I don't want the other females getting any ideas."

As Cayden watched the gentle sway of her hips as she walked away, he was struck by searing pain. He turned with a snarl to see Lucian holding up the blade that had been buried in his body not a second before.

"You could've warned me," He gritted out.

"And where would the fun have been in that?" Lucian smiled back, his dark eyes glittering as he stowed the blade in his breast pocket.

Lucian closed his eyes and seemed to concentrate. So distracted watching his odd friend, Cayden only realized they were surrounded in a sudden dense fog when Lucian, opened his eyes again.

"Now then," Lucian continued, lifting his wrist to his mouth and piercing the flesh with his fangs. Dark, syrupy blood pooled in the wound immediately. "Drink up and you'll be good as new." He held his wrist up to Cayden's lips.

"No thank you, Lucian." He shook his head, "I've heard of the effects of drinking the blood of your kind and I'd rather not- no offence."

"I only intend to heal your wounds, Cayden; I have no desire to keep you under my influence." Lucian rolled his eyes. "But I'll respect your wishes." He lowered his arm.

"Although, I am surprised. I would've thought you would like to be healed in time to see to your lady's needs tonight. I hear mating isn't overly impressive when the male is hindered by a stab wound."

Cayden snatched up Lucian's wrist and took a gulp of the warm thick liquid.

His vision blurred and his entire body felt as though it were on fire as he swallowed down the addictive substance.

"And... that should be enough." Lucian pulled his wrist away and quickly pulled down his sleeve to cover the mark.

"Damn." Cayden cursed as he held up his hand in front of his face and saw everything come into sudden sharp focus as the fog lifted just as quickly as it appeared

The rest of his senses intensified too, the conversations going on between the pack members became distinct and his nose twitched with the strength of the scents that surrounded him. Above it all, the smell of his mate was like a beacon, calling him home.

"The effects will wear off in a few hours. Now, I doubt I need to tell you that I am an incredibly private man—"

"I won't tell a soul." Cayden shook himself from his fascinated daze and looked into the endless depth of Lucian's dark eyes. "You have my word."

"Very good," Lucian said cheerfully as he prodded at Cayden's side. "Ah, you see; all better."

"Woah, Cayden you're healed," Rose said in astonishment having bounded to his side once more. She ran her hands over him, searching for his battle wounds. "What did you do?" She turned curious eyes onto Lucian.

"I merely removed the blade, my dear. You'll find that Greystones have exceptional healing abilities." Lucian smiled, took her hand in his and raised it to his lips. "It's time I bid you farewell. It was a pleasure to have met you."

"Likewise," Rose replied, slightly taken aback by

his old-world manners.

"I am assuming you would appreciate it if I were to remove this pathetic excuse for a wolf from your territory?" Lucian cocked a brow.

"If you wouldn't mind." Cayden smiled.

"Not at all, you provided a most thrilling night of entertainment, it is only fair that I repay my thanks with a favour." Lucian bowed his head gracefully. "Goodbye, Cayden."

With that, Cayden pulled on his clothes and watched as Lucian strode to where Russell was being held by members of the pack. He spoke briefly to the wolves, dismissing them with a tired wave before turning on his heel. He snapped his fingers and Cayden looked on in amazement as Russell immediately got to his feet and shuffled listlessly behind.

The Beta's eyes were glazed and fixed on some far-off point in the distance.

The rest of the pack stood just as slack-jawed as they watched Russell climb into the passenger side of the shining black sports car, his eyes still unblinking and vacant.

"I look forward to doing business with you, Mr. Greystone," Lucian called out, as he opened his door, pausing as he dipped to climb in. "And remember, I do so hate it when I miss an invitation to a mating ceremony." With a wink, he climbed in behind the wheel and with an excessive roar of the engine, he sped off into the night.

"Well, he's a strange man," Rose murmured.

"Yup. But a good one… I think." Cayden nodded with a slight frown, before turning his head to take in the beautiful sight that was his Rose.

She sighed as other pack members began to gather around them.

"I know you've got Alpha duties now, but I don't suppose you'd like to—"

"Get the hell out here?" Cayden took her hand in his and strode towards the forest path "Hell yes, Alpha duties can wait until the morning"

# CHAPTER TWENTY-TWO

*Rose*

Rose's head was spinning. On one hand, she felt giddy and elated that Cayden had not only returned but had stepped up to save her pack. Her wolf was in seventh heaven now that her mate was with her again, and Rose couldn't blame her for having rolled over and forgiven him for leaving in the first place. She herself had been swept up in the moment and had let her relief and joy at having Cayden back, smother her hurt and anger at what he had done.

Now, with him taking a shower in her small bathroom, she had a moment to breathe and to think clearly.

She was undoubtedly pleased that he was back, and she knew she wanted him to stay. She still wanted him as her mate, but she needed answers. Perhaps he had a good reason for leaving her, but until she knew what had happened with him, she wasn't sure she would be able to let herself trust him. She wanted to. She knew he was a good wolf, but the prickle of doubt in her mind whispered that there was a chance that he might leave her again.

She had changed out of her friend's pretty pink mating dress and pulled the pins out of her hair, letting it fall loose. She gently rubbed at her scalp in relief, wondering why women regularly put themselves through such torture. She stared into the mirror and let out an amused snort at her reflection. Her make-up had run, making her resemble something out of a horror movie. She scrubbed at her face with a cleansing wipe and pulled on her soft and comfortable pyjamas.

Feeling more like herself again she padded to the kitchen to fix herself a hot tea. As she stirred her drink she sensed, rather than heard Cayden's approach. His clean fresh scent tickled her nose, and she could almost feel the warmth from his body. It would be easy to just take him by the hand and fall into bed with him, but in the morning, she'd still have the same questions and doubts running through her head.

Rose turned and let her eyes track down over his sculpted body. He stood there in her kitchen wearing just a towel wrapped around his hips, his chest glistening from his shower. He sure was one delicious specimen, her body's reaction to him was undeniable. But by the slightly uncertain look in his eyes, she knew he had been thinking the same thing as her. They needed to talk.

"Did you want some tea?" She asked quietly, cursing herself for beginning with such a dumb question.

Cayden shook his head and smiled softly at her.

"I'm good."

Rose nodded and gestured to the couch, before lightly stepping around him. The temptation to drop a quick kiss on his lips as she passed was not something she could give in to. Not until she had her answers.

Cayden followed quietly behind and joined her on her couch. She clutched her mug of tea tightly in front of her, using it as a shield.

"So, I guess we need to talk." Cayden began, resting his elbows on his knees as he leaned forward in his seat.

"We do."

They both sighed and stared at the same spot on the ground. Before she lost her courage, Rose decided to rip the bandaid off.

"Why did you leave me, Cayden?"

He scrubbed a hand over his face and turned to look at her.

"I thought I was doing what was best for you."

"Why did you think you could make that decision for me?" She countered.

"I know." He agreed, "I should've spoken with you, but at the time I was afraid."

"Afraid of what?"

"That you'd convince me not to go, convince me that I deserved you. I couldn't risk giving in to what we have between us. A mating bond like this tore my family apart. Turned my father into an abusive monster. I was afraid that history would repeat itself."

"So, you thought you were protecting me from yourself? Cayden the best way to protect someone is to love them enough to give them honesty. Instead, by keeping how you felt from me, you've hurt me. You've hurt me more than I ever thought possible. Now, I don't know if I can be certain that you won't hurt me again."

"I know." Cayden sighed sadly and placed his hand on her knee. "I'm so sorry, Rose. I never wanted to hurt you. I was wrong. I realize that now. But in my warped view of things, I thought I was loving you in the best way I could. By letting you go, so you could find safety and happiness elsewhere. I was so convinced that after the initial attraction levelled out, you'd never have happiness with me. I'm a lone wolf. I have no connections, I live from paycheck to paycheck, I move around for work and I live out of a truck and a trailer." He cursed shaking his head, "Well, I used to. Russell burned down my trailer and Lucian had my truck towed, so now I have jack-shit to my name."

Tears welled in her eyes as she finally saw the broken man that sat in front of her. He might appear strong, confident, big and bad, but he was filled with self-loathing and low esteem. He was for once, completely bare to her. His flaws on show and vulnerable. While she might've been hurt and angry with him, the love for him that flooded her was all-consuming.

"Cayden, I don't want you for your job, I don't want you for your home or the car you drive. I want you because you are a good wolf, who stands up for what is right and puts the needs of others above his own. You care for people, showing them kindness and consideration when you rarely get the same in return. I want to be your mate because I love you Cayden, and I know you love me back."

He raised disbelieving eyes to meet hers.

"But Rose, if you mate me, you'd be a lone wolf. You'd have to say goodbye to your grandmother, your friends, your home, to everything you've ever known and loved. We'd be on the road constantly;

shunned by other packs."

Rose frowned and put her tea down on her coffee table.

"Aren't you forgetting that you're not a lone wolf anymore? You're Alpha of Darkhills now, we don't need to go anywhere. Our home can be here."

Cayden shook his head and looked away again.

"I wasn't fit to lead before, my father said I was a disgrace, that all I would ever do is hurt people, that I didn't deserve to be an Alpha. And he was right, I hurt you Rose, the one person I should protect and cherish above all else. I'm not fit to remain as the Darkhills Alpha."

"Your father was so very wrong about you Cayden, one day I hope you'll be able to see that. You acted how you did because you thought you were protecting me." Rose countered.

"And look how well it turned out," Cayden said bitterly. "I hurt you anyway and put you in even greater danger."

"OK, and then what happened?" Rose asked, "You came back, you fought to protect me, and you have apologized to me."

"I'll always fight for you Rose, but I'll never be what you or the pack deserves. I'll never be a perfect Alpha."

She took his hands and forced him to look at her again.

"Cayden, I don't need you to be a perfect male or a perfect Alpha, I need you to be honest with me. And Darkhills needs honesty too. Hell, we've all lived with so much deceit and blackmail for far too long. What this pack deserves is a wolf with your compassion, fairness and integrity."

"I promise to be honest with you from now on Rose, I—"

"Good," Rose interrupted him, holding up a hand to silence the protest that she didn't doubt was on the tip of his tongue. "So, answer me honestly now: Do you love me?"

"Yes, with every fibre of my being," Cayden answered, his amber eyes burning into hers.

"Do you want me to be happy?"

"More than anything."

"Then will you please stop being so self-sacrificing and mate me already?" She asked with an exasperated sigh. "I love you, Cayden Greystone, and I don't care if you are a lone wolf, an Alpha or a man without a penny to his name, I want to be with *you*."

Cayden's lips tilted up in the smallest of smiles

and Rose had never seen a sweeter thing in her life.

"I know you see yourself a certain way because of your upbringing and that it will take time for you to see things the way everyone else does, the way I do, but I promise you, you are worth every bit of my love."

"Then for you, Rose, I will work every day of my life to try to be the man you deserve, and the Alpha Darkhills needs."

Cayden took a deep breath and dropped to one knee in front of where she sat on the couch.

"I love you, Rose Woods, I never thought I'd be so lucky as to deserve a female as perfect as you. Please, would you do me the honour of becoming my mate?" His amber eyes shone with sincerity.

"Yes, you big, bad idiot!" She threw her arms around his neck and pressed her lips against his.

"Are you sure Rose?" Cayden asked as he got to his feet, taking her with him in his arms, "I can't promise that I won't mess up again, or that—"

"Yes, I'm sure! Now would you hurry up and take me to bed already?" Rose clamped her hand down on his mouth with a grin.

His eyes blazed and lit with need as he strode with her in his arms into her bedroom.

"With pleasure." He growled as he threw her lightly down onto the mattress.

Rose giggled, as he launched himself at her, tugging her up the bed so her head lay on the pillows. Her laughter ceased as soon as his lips closed around hers. Instead of the fiery blaze of passion that she had expected he peppered her lips, cheeks and eyelids, with feather-soft kisses. Rose sighed happily as she basked in his love.

"My Rose, my beautiful Rose."

Cayden continued to trail kisses down her neck, slipping the thin strap of her camisole to the side so he could continue his path across her skin. She gasped as his fingers gently grazed down her side.

"Cayden, please don't torture me again," She begged, already desperate to be one with him.

"Tell me what you want, Rose," He purred as he slid her camisole lower and gently sucked her nipple into his mouth.

Her back arched, as she desperately sought more of the sensations he was giving her.

"I want you, inside me." She groaned.

He chuckled softly, giving her puckered tip a small nip with his teeth.

"Then we had better get rid of these." He sat back and flicked out a claw as he eyed her wickedly.

With a few careful slices of fabric, her clothes fell away from her body.

"Sorry if you liked those, but I think you'll prefer being without them." With that, he pulled the clothes away from beneath her and tossed them across the room.

He grasped her thighs and spread her before him, his eyes heating with desire. God, she loved how he looked at her, just a look was enough to flood her with arousal. He bent his head low and inhaled deeply at her core, groaning his satisfaction.

"Your scent drives me wild, Rose." He opened his eyes and shot her with a look of molten desire. "And your taste," He slowly ran the flat of his tongue up her slit and over her sensitive nub, both of them moaning in unison. "You taste like heaven."

With that he lowered his mouth to her clit, licking and sucking it into his mouth in a demanding rhythm that left Rose gasping for breath as an orgasm struck her.

She cried out his name, her hands finding purchase in his hair as she rocked her hips against his mouth.

Cayden growled and lifted her so he could grasp her ass and pull her onto his tongue as he dipped low into her core. The hot, wet lapping sensation had her moaning again as she helplessly gave herself over to the deep, pulsing pleasure that was building within her.

Rose opened her eyes and felt another surging climax rising within her. She watched the erotic sight of her huge and powerful mate, lost in rapture as he feasted like he'd never get enough of having her on his tongue.

She came apart with a low moan of greedy satisfaction, her hips rolling of their own volition as Cayden gently lowered her to the mattress. He placed hot, wet kisses down her thighs as he pulled back to remove the towel from around his hips.

"Mine." The possessive growl left her throat as she eyed his thick manhood.

"Yours." Cayden husked as he gripped himself, his eyes locked on hers.

"Tell me if you've changed your mind, Rose," he whispered.

Her reply was to reach forward and wrap her hand around him. He shuddered in her hand as she stroked the velvety smooth shaft. Rose suddenly felt like the most powerful woman in the world as she watched his head tip back and a grunt of pleasure leave his lips.

"God, Rose."

She worked her hand a little faster and squeezed ever so slightly, enjoying how his breath hitched.

"Look at me, Cayden," she purred at him, her Luna voice filtering through the lust-filled haze in the room.

His eyes immediately found hers, a look of astonishment and need burning hot in his gaze.

"Do I look like I've changed my mind?" She licked her lips and bent her head towards him.

"Oh fuck." Cayden cursed as she licked the head of him.

Her playtime was swiftly over as she found herself hauled up and tossed back on the bed, Cayden's body pressed firmly against hers. She eagerly pulled her knees up so he could rest the thick head of his cock against the entrance of her sex.

"Cayden, please," her plea ended with a sigh as he slowly thrust his hips forward, filling her.

When he was fully seated inside her, they both gasped and stared into each other's eyes. Love and desire coursed through her as she felt Cayden's heart beating firmly against her own.

Keeping his eyes locked on hers, he began to move. Each withdrawal and thrust lit her up with the most delicious sensation of slick friction. Her body clenched around him and with a pleasured groan he upped his thrusts until their hips were meeting in a carnal and hungry rhythm. A climax that threatened to drown her in ecstasy crested within her, with every deep thrust from her mate she whimpered with the need to fall into the pleasurable abyss that awaited her.

Cayden roared as his need to claim his mate overcame him. He bit down hard upon her neck, his canines sinking into the tender flesh, causing her orgasm to finally break, flooding her with wave after wave of blinding pleasure.

Her body pulled and clutched at her mate as spirals of never-ending release poured through her, her teeth extended, and she bit down hard on his muscular shoulder. His body stiffened as he spilled into her tight heat with a loan moan of abandonment, sending her into another rolling swell of bliss.

They pulled their heads back and stared at one another, their lips stained slightly with each other's blood. Their mouths collided between harsh breaths in the aftermath of their mating. Their kiss slowed to soft licks and caresses as their bodies relaxed and their heartbeats slowed to the same steady rhythm.

Cayden rolled off her, pulling her across his chest, as they both lay there catching their breath. Rose glanced up at his shoulder and smiled as she saw the mating mark she had given him already healing to a light silvery scar.

She couldn't wait to inspect hers in the mirror later. She snuggled into his chest and placed a kiss over his heart with a softly whispered, 'I love you.'

"I love you, my Rose," he sighed in happy exhaustion.

Tomorrow they would face the rest of their future together. It would be difficult at times, and there was a lot of work to do to restore the Darkhills pack to the happy and thriving community that it once was, but Rose knew they were both up for the challenge. As long as they were together, there was nothing they couldn't face.

# EPILOGUE

## *Cayden*

Cayden climbed out of his new pickup, grabbing the architect's blueprints from the side seat as he went.

The plans to re-purpose the old Alpha's large townhouse as a boutique hotel were looking good. He needed to get his interior design experts to take a look over a few samples that the architect had suggested but, he was certain they would already have an idea of what the place needed. He'd bring it up after dinner that evening, Rose was looking forward to hosting her best friend and his Beta for dinner.

He strode up the porch steps of the old Woods house and smiled as he saw Judy perched on a chair in the kitchen, regaling his mate with some cringe-worthy story while her carer shook his head ruefully. The elder might be weaker in body after the incident a few months back, but her wit and sense of humour were as strong as ever.

"I don't wanna hear it, Judy," Cayden called out as he walked into his new home, depositing his keys and the blueprints on the sideboard. "These sensitive ears of mine can't take one more of your wild stories."

Rose beamed up at him as he wrapped an arm

around her waist, pulling her in for a kiss.

"Oh, Cayden darlin', as if I could say anything to make someone blush," Judy replied.

"Mmm hmm, I'm not sure Thomas here would agree." Cayden sent the young man who acted as the elder's carer a conspiratorial glance.

"My day is never dull, Mr. Greystone and that's all I'll say on the matter."

"You see! I'm just trying to keep the boy entertained is all." Judy laughed merrily, holding up her hands in mock innocence.

"How's the hotel coming on?" Rose asked, her eyes sparkling with excitement.

"Good, got some more plans to go over this evening."

Rose rolled her eyes at that. Admittedly, he did tend to bring his work home most evenings. Being Alpha wasn't a nine-to-five job, but he found he liked being busy, he liked working toward something that would benefit others.

"But I promise all it'll be is deciding on floor samples, which I know you and Carly already have some ideas about. While you're talking flooring, Clint and I will figure out the proportions for the cabins going up in the hills. We won't be talking shop *all* night."

"Don't he ever stop?" Judy nudged Rose. "You'll burn yourself out if you carry on like this." She wagged a finger in Cayden's face, which he snapped at playfully, making the old lady jump and tsk at him.

"I'll stop in about seven months."

Cayden dropped down to his knees and nuzzled into his mate's only slightly rounded stomach.

"I want to have things in a good place for when I take some time off to care for these two."

Rose beamed down at him, her eyes shining with pure joy. He may not have had the best role model, but he sure as hell wasn't going to let his past interfere with his determination to be the best dad he could be to his cub.

"Gran's got a point, Cayden; I don't want you tiring yourself out." She sent him a suggestive wink and his wolf growled.

His mate had been voracious in the bedroom lately. She blamed the hormones. Cayden didn't care what it was, just as long as he was able to make her scream every night, he was one happy wolf.

"Poor Thomas! Look what you two have gone and done. Why, the boy is about to combust." Judy called out, throwing her hands in the air. "Come on now, dear, I think it's about time we left these two deviants and headed back."

The carer chuckled and held out his arm ready to assist her.

"Bye Gran, you want to come for lunch next week?" Rose embraced her grandmother with a happy squeeze.

"You bet, I gotta show you how to make berry cobbler, just the way your grandfather liked it." Judy kissed her on the nose and cupped Cayden by the cheek. "You take care of my girl now, Cayden you hear?"

"Yes Ma'am, you can count on it."

He stood with his arms around his mate on the porch as they waved goodbye to Judy. She had insisted on gifting him and Rose the house in the woods so they could raise a new generation there in the family home. She seemed more than happy in her new retirement apartment in the centre of town, especially considering she got to tease the hired help.

"I finally got a reply from Lucian today," Rose said absently as she rested her head back against his chest. "Looks like he's bringing a date to the mating ceremony."

"You're kidding."

"Nope. I can't wait to meet whoever she is. Did

you know he was dating someone?"

"Not a clue, all I know is that he does 'so love a mating ceremony,'" Cayden responded, putting on his best British accent, making his mate laugh even if he did get swatted for it.

"So, that's all the guests confirmed," He chuckled, wrapping his arms around her tightly, rubbing his hands gently over her stomach.

"Yup, you still feeling OK about having the Greystone Alpha and Luna join us?" Rose asked, looking cautiously over her shoulder at him.

"Absolutely. It's time some wounds were healed."

She turned in his arms and leaned up on her tiptoes to kiss him sweetly.

"I love you, Cayden Greystone."

"And I love you, my Rose, but I've got a question for you."

She looked up at him with her beguiling green eyes that saw him for all that he was.

"How much time have we got before Clint and Carly arrive for dinner?"

Her expression turned into one of mischievous intent.

"Oh, at least an hour or so." Rose grinned at him.

He swept her up into his arms eliciting a squeal of delight from his mate. With his Rose safely tucked against his chest, Cayden marched with her back into their home.

"I'm sure I can work with that."

# THANK YOU

Thank you gor reading Saved By The Big Bad Wolf, the first in the Darkhills Romance Series. I hope you enjoyed Cayden and Rose's story as much as I enjoyed writing it.

The support of my readers is so appreciated, I love hearing from you and having your feedback so I can keep creating characters and stories that you will enjoy.

By leaving a short review you can help me share my stories with more people like you, so if you're feeling kind, please pen me a little something. I guarantee you'll make my day. Who knows- you might prompt a little happy dance.

Don't forget to check out the next in the Darkhills series, Escaping the Beast, featuring the mysterious and brooding Lord Lucian Nightingale.

◆ ◆ ◆

# BOOKS IN THIS SERIES

## *The Darkhills Series*

Darkhills Romance Series A series of standalone paranormal romance stories that guarantee action, adventure and steamy scenes that will make your toes curl.

While the books can be read in any order, it is recommended that readers begin with Saved by the Big Bad Wolf, as some characters cross over.

Happily Ever Afters guaranteed.

## **Saved By The Big Bad Wolf**

Raised by her grandparents, Rose Woods has lived a safe and steady life as a member of the Darkhills wolf pack. When her place within the pack is under threat, she is faced with an impossible choice:

Mate the Alpha or leave.

All seems lost until she is forced to defy pack law and go on the run with a mysterious and dangerously enthralling lone wolf.

Cayden Greystone is the rightful Alpha of the Greystone pack, but past tragedies have convinced him he is better off alone. That is until he meets Rose. When she's threatened, his wolf's need to protect and claim his mate has dire repercussions for them both.

Will the strength of their bond be enough to save them, or will pack covenants and past demons prevent a new moon rising for the Darkhills pack?

Saved by the Big Bad Wolf is the first in a paranormal romance series from Elizabeth Greene. If you like stories that feature action, adventure, feisty heroines and hot as hell heroes that leave you tingling in all the right places, then you'll love what is waiting for you in the Darkhills.

Intended for an 18+ audience, this story contains steamy sex scenes, scenes of violence and some strong language.
Trigger warning: This story contains mention of sexual assault but is not explored in any detail.

## Escaping The Beast

This was the last time, she vowed.

Never again would she settle his debts or give him

an alibi... she had said the same thing the last time, and the time before that.

When Katherine was summoned to help her charlatan father with his latest business deal, she convinced herself to go to her old man's rescue. She was, after all, studying to become a lawyer and assisting him with the terms of a contract should've been a walk in the park.

What she hadn't expected, however, was that a deal had already been struck: her freedom had been sacrificed for her father's. Determined not to act the victim or let her poker face slip, she finds herself negotiating terms with the devil himself.

One thing she is absolutely certain of; she won't let her heart become part of the negotiations. Even if there is something about the dark and dangerous Lucian Nightingale that calls to her.

Lord Lucian Nightingale was preparing to leave the Darkhills to seek new distractions from the void of his long, immortal existence. Deciding to tie up loose ends, he agrees to an unconventional proposition from a man who owes him a large debt.

He never expected to fall for the woman who strode into his mansion like she owned the place. Drawn in by her intelligence, stubbornness and false confidence, Lucian finds himself compelled to know her better and quickly becomes determined to win Katherine's trust and heart.

If he can do that, perhaps he can prove that he is not the beast that he first appears to be, and she might hold the key to banishing the loneliness that haunts him.

Escaping the Beast is a vampire paranormal romance and is the second in the Darkhills series. While each story can be read as a standalone, readers may wish to also read the earlier book: 'Saved By The Big Bad Wolf'. Each book comes with a Happy Ever After.

This beauty and the beast inspired, vampire PNR contains steamy love scenes and some crude language. Recommended for an 18+ audience.

## Broken Slumber

Her heart thumped and her body ached as the forest scratched and clawed at her, but there was no way she could possibly stop.

Brianna St. Clare was running for her life, of that she was certain. The problem was, she had no memory of what she was running from.

A dragon shifter's lair becomes the perfect place to hide, and there's no better creature to protect her from the repercussions of her past crimes, than a dragon.

As the two of them try to piece together the gaps in her memory, Brianna finds herself drawn to a man with whom she couldn't be more different. She wants her life back, but some of the dragon's possessiveness is rubbing off on her, and now she's wondering if she can keep what is hers.

Etienne tasted her fear on the wind and his dragon demanded he act.

Having rescued a lost and frightened woman in the woods, he may have found a new purpose for living.

However, she is a journalist who had her memory wiped because she planned to expose the paranormal world. Is his dragon's fascination with the woman preventing him from doing what he should, to protect others like him?

All he knows is, his drive to possess, protect and pleasure the woman will either save or destroy him.

Broken Slumber is a dragon shifter paranormal romance and is the third in the Darkhills series. While each story can be read as a standalone, readers may wish to also read the earlier books:

'Saved By The Big Bad Wolf' and 'Escaping The Beast'. Each book comes with a Happy Ever After.

This slow-burn, BWWM PNR contains steamy love scenes and some crude language. Recommended for an 18+ audience.

## Choosing Her Mate

It was only supposed to be one night, one final moment of selfish indulgence. She never expected to find her True Mate. She never meant to mark him as hers.

As the next in line to a prestigious family of bear shifters, Doctor Samantha Rivers always knew she would need to mate strategically for the good of her family and with her father's rapidly declining health, her time was up.

An arranged marriage was her future, she had made her peace with that long ago, but as The Choosing Ceremony is announced, her heart refuses to forget the male who was fated for her.

Life was simple. Benson Pines fought, got paid then sent the money to his sister. There was never any point in dreaming of something more, that was until he needed to check in to the hospital.

He didn't believe in Insta-Love, or love at first sight; lust at first sight, was as real as it got. At least, so he thought. One chance encounter with the commanding and beautiful Dr. Rivers and all bets were off.

He found his mate; the only problem was, the next morning she was gone.

If he wants her back, rough and ready Benson needs to step out of his comfort zone and compete in a high society dating game. It's a good thing his bear isn't one to shy away from a fight because he's not giving up on Happily Ever After; he just needs to convince his mate that she can fight for it too.

Fairy tale meets dating pageant with this fun, action-packed, steamy love story. This unique twist on 'Goldilocks and the Three Bears' will become your new favourite PNR.

Choosing Her Mate is the fourth book in the Darkhills Romance Series and follows the unorthodox path to love for two bear shifters.

While each story in the Darkhills series can be read as a standalone, readers may wish to also read the earlier books: 'Saved By The Big Bad Wolf', 'Escaping

The Beast' and 'Broken Slumber'. Each book comes with a Happy Ever After guarantee.

Choosing Her Mate contains steamy love scenes and some crude language. Recommended for an 18+ audience.

## Mannequin Mates

She was not running away. She most definitely was not run— Okay, so, to an observer it might've looked like she was running away, but a fresh start somewhere new was exactly what was needed to escape the never-ending cycle of manipulation from her friend and ex-boss.

Imogen had plans. Plans that would see her little business blossom and thrive as she puts her inherent talents to good use, creating beautiful clothes for an ever-growing list of paranormal clients. Darkhills was calling, and she was eager to make the move for a simpler, happier way of life.

Stumbling upon two handsome and protective elven warriors that make her insides do happy little flip-flops, was not part of the plan. Nor was discovering a demon was out to get her, but Imogen wasn't about to let a little thing like that get in her way, especially when it turns out she isn't as defenceless as she once thought.

Embarking on an unexpected path of self-discovery with her elves, Imogen is determined to make it out of the city alive. She only prays her heart can survive.

Derion and River are two elven warriors on a mission: to protect humankind from the threat of demonic attack. Tasked with banishing a demon hellbent on unknown levels of pain and destruction, the two heroes take to the city streets to hunt their foe.

When the demon's intended victim, a petite and enthralling woman, forces her way into their operation, the pair of elven warriors soon realise there is more to her than meets the eye.

Their battle against the forces of Hell becomes personal when neither elf can ignore their attraction towards the woman. They can only hope they have what it takes to protect their intended bride and convince her of where her future lies: with them.

Fairy tale meets urban fantasy with this fun, action-packed, steamy love story. This unique twist on the classic 'Elves and the Shoemaker' story, will become your new favourite Paranormal Romance.

Mannequin Mates is the fifth book in the Darkhills Romance Series and follows a, potentially more than human, fashionista on a path of self-discovery with two handsome and sinfully seductive elven warriors.

While each story in the Darkhills series can be read as a standalone, readers may wish to also read the earlier books: 'Saved By The Big Bad Wolf', 'Escaping The Beast', 'Broken Slumber' and 'Choosing Her Mate' as some characters will overlap from previous stories. Each book comes with a Happy Ever After guarantee.

Mannequin Mates contains steamy love scenes, including ménage à trois, crude language and some threats of violence. Recommended for an 18+ audience.

## Mated Against The Odds

Rose Woods is about to have everything she ever dreamed of. Heavily pregnant, she can't wait to officially claim Cayden Greystone as her mate and take on the mantle of leadership as Luna of the Darkhills wolf pack.

But between constant wedding planning disasters and her mate's extreme moodiness, Rose can't help but consider herself cursed and is struggling to feel excited about the big day.

When it becomes clear that there is something more sinister at play than simply bad luck, Rose finds herself faced with another fight to secure her Happily Ever After.

Her mate is suffering, his tight self-control splintering, but Rose won't let Cayden face what plagues his mind, alone. This time, she is determined they will face their enemies together.


Cayden Greystone has a lot going on. Being Alpha of the Darkhills wolf-shifter pack hasn't been the easiest of rides and it only seems to be getting worse.

There's a suffocating presence within him, taunting him and feeding upon his worst fears. The dark whispering voice in his head takes cruel delight in triggering his inner wolf's aggressive nature and Cayden's starting to question if he's truly worthy of being Rose's mate.

If he can't keep his violent and destructive thoughts under control, he could hurt those he loves the most, and that's a risk he simply cannot take.

When Cayden discovers a past enemy is making a resurgence, hellbent on destroying everything he's ever held dear, all bets are off. There is nothing the Alpha of the Darkhills pack won't do, no demon he won't face, to protect his mate and unborn child.

Mated Against The Odds is a wolf-shifter paranormal romance. It is the sixth in the Darkhills series and revisits Rose and Cayden, from the first book within the series, as they fight for their future together.

While each story within the series can be read as a standalone, readers may wish to also read the earlier books, particularly 'Saved By The Big Bad Wolf' (Book 1), as the same main characters feature in addition to other characters from previous books. Each book within the Darkhills Series comes with a Happy Ever After.

This story includes pregnancy, childbirth, a protective Alpha Baby-Daddy, a fierce and caring female main character, steamy sex scenes, scenes of violence and some strong language. Recommended for an 18+ audience.

Trigger warning: This story contains mention of sexual assault but is not explored in any detail.

# SNEAK PREVIEW:

# ESCAPING THE BEAST

## *Lucian*

Lord Lucian Nightingale looked out of the french doors that led onto the balcony of his private suite and wondered at the rain. It seemed to fall in heavy slow motion this evening. Each drop against the glass panes punctuation for something. He was used to seeing things move slowly around him. Slowing his pace to fit with the rhythm of everything else, had long since become second nature to him, and yet sometimes when he became lost in his own thoughts, moments like this would catch him off guard. The rain was particularly heavy and plentiful. Perhaps it was just a mere optical illusion that he, being what he was, was more prone to notice.

His phone vibrated in the inside pocket of his tailored suit jacket, drawing his focus back to the present. He absently reached inside the silk lining and slid the shining screen out. It was a message from his associate, or rather he supposed, he should say, friend.

> *Cayden: There is a young woman on her way to Tumbricane. You expecting her?*

Lucian sighed. Indeed he was expecting her.

> *Lucian: She has been requested by a man with whom I have business. All is well Mr Greystone.*

He was about to return his phone to its resting place when it vibrated again in his hand.

> *Cayden: Alright then. By the way, Rose wants to know if you're planning on coming to our mating ceremony?*

He smiled a little at that and slid his phone back in his pocket. He would send a formal reply within the next week or so. He was undecided as to whether he would attend. While he liked the Alpha and Luna of the Darkhills pack and he would enjoy being amongst others for a night, he knew there would be a bittersweetness to the whole affair that would likely send him into a downward spiral.

He would never be able to have what Cayden and his mate Rose had. Someone to love and to cherish and put above all others. Someone to raise a family and grow old with. He was playing a dangerous enough game as it was by courting a friendship with the Alpha. He would have to watch as the wolf shifter grew old and eventually withered and died. But he couldn't stop himself from wanting something of an interaction with another living being. Cayden was a good man. He was dutiful, honest, trustworthy, and loyal. He was exactly how Lucian himself had been. How he had tried to remain for so long before he had woken up to the reality of what he truly was.

It would be better if he avoided contact with others for a while. Perhaps a period of solitude might suit him well. It would likely be considered rude but it was probably for the best that he left Cayden and Rose to celebrate their nuptials with those who could live and grow with them. He wouldn't flatter himself to think that the Alpha would be upset by his absence, but it would likely put his keen nose out of joint.

He returned his gaze to the rain once again. The

sound of it on the panes of glass lulling him into a calm and contemplative state. He was never sure which was better for his mood. To spend time within the city so he could observe the virility of life at a detached distance or remain in the quiet solitude of his estate in the foothills of the mountains. It seemed as though wherever he resided he was becoming more prone to bouts of loneliness. Perhaps after the nasty business with Mr. Daxton was finished he would look to emigrate elsewhere. He hadn't visited his British homeland since he left centuries ago, and yet he still couldn't bring himself to return. Perhaps a tour of Europe would enliven him enough to keep the darkness at bay?

He suddenly became aware of tingling at the back of his neck and turned his head slightly towards the source of his interruption. Lucian sensed the lost soul of his manservant before he knocked quietly on the door to his chambers. The poor man had once been so torn apart by grief at losing his family, that he had come to Lucian to beg for them to be returned to him.

Many wrongly thought he was capable of raising the dead. But alas, he was no necromancer. He had felt pity for the man whose mind, heart and soul were utterly destroyed. He'd offered him peace instead and existence without pain. The butler lived permanently under Lucian's thrall. Living comfortably at Tumbricane, and attending to Lucian with small duties to keep his mind from rotting.

"My lord, Mr. Pines and your guest Mr. Daxton are assembled in the Hall. It is nearly midnight." The monosyllabic voice spoke softly behind him.

"Very good. I will join them shortly. Thank you, Mr. Jones."

The shuffling of the man's feet grew quieter as he retreated down the hallway.

Lucian sighed. Time to see if the despicable Mr. Daxton really would have his only daughter take his place, while he tried to find the finances required to settle his debt.

When the man had first requested Lucian's assistance with the notoriously sadistic mob overlords to whom he was indebted, he had felt pity for the man. He had played a fine fiddle and Lucian had paid off his debts and consolidated them into one. When it became apparent that Kyle Daxton was avoiding making any repayments, Lucian had requested they meet to re-negotiate terms. It had taken weeks for the man to be persuaded to face Lucian again. When he had arrived four months ago, he had been desperate and had tried to demand an increased loan so that he could invest it in a 'sure thing' and make them both rich men.

Lucian didn't need to be made a rich man. He already was one. He refused the man's offer and suggested he pay out his debt through servitude to him. For the past few months, Kyle Daxton had lived at Tumbricane in comfort while he considered the proposition. Lucian understood that the man felt that this was unfair imprisonment, but he had been provided with a comfortable room, within which he could move about freely. He was given three good meals a day and if he at any point wished to accept Lucian's offer, he would be allowed to have contact with others.

When he had requested a meeting the previous night, Lucian thought he was finally going to agree to undertake employment. What he didn't expect was the man to negotiate, offering Lucian his adult daughter to stay at Tumbricane in his stead, while he got Lucian his money. Intrigued as to whether he would truly go through with such a plan, Lucian had agreed. Perhaps the incentive of returning for his daughter would be what was required to get the man to square his finances once and for all.

Lucian strode from his chambers and in a flash

swept down the hidden stairwell that led to the great hall below. He appeared as a blur of movement as he slid out from behind the heavy tapestry that covered the wall and graciously sat in his chair that formed the centrepiece of the room. He watched as the nervous-looking Mr. Daxton had visibly paled at his sudden appearance.

The man must've had an inkling as to what Lucian was, but was most likely too frightened to say it out loud. Frightened of sounding like a madman and frightened that it was true. Beside him stood the man whom Lucian had hired as a guard for Mr. Daxton. Lucian suspected he had no idea that he'd been under guard while staying at Tumbricane, but Lucian had ensured he was kept abreast of the man's fruitless attempts to escape during the day.

Mr. Benson Pines had never had to intervene, but he remained ready to act should it be required. Lucian had originally thought to hire the new Darkhills Alpha for the task, but it hadn't worked out that way. Instead, the brutally capable bear shifter had proved to be a worthy replacement.

Lucian raised his hand and silently beckoned the two men forward. The difference between their gaits almost comical as the man hurried forward as though his coattails were on fire, whereas the bear shifter simply ate up the ground in long confident strides.

"Good evening, gentlemen," Lucian began. "You both understand why you are here. Mr. Pines, please may I extend to you my thanks thus far. I am certain you will continue to prove useful to me. Please keep me informed as to how matters progress, as previously discussed."

The bear shifter nodded silently and turned and left. Lucian would receive updates regarding how Kyle Daxton was progressing with his plans to settle his debts. He would be followed and watched from afar by the hired man and, if at any point Lucian felt it were necessary, Mr. Pines would be instructed to apprehend him.

"What about me? Am I free to go now?" The obnoxious voice of Kyle Daxton broke through the silence.

Lucian wondered how someone who appeared so nervous and on edge, could manage to sound so entitled.

"Not yet Mr. Daxton. We are awaiting your daughter's arrival, are we not?"

"Of course, of course." He nodded, "You're gonna really love her. You'll be pleased to know she gets her looks from her mother." Kyle laughed, as though they were on friendly terms.

Lucian ignored him. The way the young woman looked was of no consequence to him. She would be well cared for while in his home, he was a gentleman and did not believe in punishing others for the actions of their kin. He would not prolong the young lady's visit here for any longer than necessary. Lucian had already decided upon a timescale in his mind. Mr. Daxton had three months to repay his debt, or he would be returning to Tumbricane once more.

"I mean she's real pretty, got a big pair of titties on her. Just like her mother did."

Lucian fixed the man with a withering look that told him to stop talking. Unfortunately, the idiotic man didn't seem to know how to shut up.

"You know my ex-wife used to dance on the strip in Vegas. That's where we met you know, I was the high roller and she was the prettiest piece of eye candy you ever saw. My kitty-kat could be just as good if she let loose a little bit. Not that she's not fun, but you know she's-"

"Mr. Daxton I believe now would be a good time to desist."

"Okay, okay. Sure, sure. I mean it's getting close to midnight and I'm thinking maybe she's gotten lost or something, so perhaps I should head outside and see if I can't find her-"

"Enough." Lucian held up a hand and summoned his will to command Kyle to fall silent. He didn't like to use his abilities unnecessarily, but there were times when he would make an exception.

The silence that hung in the air was golden and Lucian breathed it in deeply. It didn't last long, however, as the low rumble of an engine could be heard as it approached.

Kyle looked over his shoulder at the sound and winked at Lucian. Not for the first time while having been subjected to Mr. Daxton's company, did Lucian consider whether it would have been better for him to be the beast most people thought him to be. He wondered whether it would be easier and better for everyone involved if he were to just kill the man where he stood. Alas, he preferred to avoid violence wherever possible.

The slow shuffling steps of the butler approached the door and Lucian sat back in his chair. Mr. Daxton had said that his daughter got her looks from her mother. Lucian found himself hoping she had also avoided inheriting her father's personality. The sound of the engine cutting off and a quiet thud of a car door being shut, made Lucian's eyes track to the entrance. With slight apprehension, he awaited the arrival of the much-promised Miss. Daxton.

Printed in Great Britain
by Amazon